FERAL

There's something not quite right about Shelby's Oasis, the tourist trap in the middle of the Arizona desert. The Shelby sisters, Agnes and Diana, have more skeletons than closets in which to hide them. And with rumours of a fortune in gold buried on the property, who can be trusted — the sisters' scheming brother Scott? The seductive Kelly-Anne? Or Mitch, the loner who stumbles into their lives? One thing's for sure: nothing at Shelby's Oasis is what it seems . . .

STEVE HAYES
AND
DAVID WHITEHEAD

───────────◆───────────

FERAL

Complete and Unabridged

LINFORD
Leicester

First published in Great Britain

First Linford Edition
published 2010

British Library CIP Data

Hayes, Steve.
  Feral. - - (Linford mystery library)
  1. Resorts- -Arizona- -Fiction. 2. Treasure
troves- -Fiction. 3. Suspense fiction.
  4. Large type books.
  I. Title II. Series III. Whitehead, David,
  1958 –
  823.9′2–dc22

ISBN 978–1–44480–144–6

Published by
F. A. Thorpe (Publishing)
Anstey, Leicestershire

Set by Words & Graphics Ltd.
Anstey, Leicestershire
Printed and bound in Great Britain by
T. J. International Ltd., Padstow, Cornwall

This book is printed on acid-free paper

1

The slow-moving desert tortoise was at least half a century old.

Now, roughly halfway through his life and therefore in his prime, the key elements of his unhurried existence were food, sleep and the need to breed almost constantly from one fall to the next.

Hauling himself up off the loose, dun-coloured sand with his stubby, paddle-like front legs, he began to cross a dirt road that cut through the wilderness like a half-healed scar, the small, blunt head on his scrawny neck turning to neither left nor right, but staring fixedly straight ahead.

He had only one thought in mind: to feast on the succulent new growth of the teddy bear cholla that grew in abundance on the other side of the trail.

Thus, he was entirely unaware of the red Ford pickup speeding towards him from the southwest.

The first he knew of it was when he sensed vibration in the hot ground beneath his belly, faint at first but growing steadily more insistent.

Even then he still kept propelling himself inch by inch toward the middle of the road, straight into its path.

Too late it occurred to him to turn his golf ball-sized head toward the growing snarl of the engine. By then, the truck was coming so fast that it looked more like a red smudge than a solid shape in the dancing heat waves.

The tortoise had time to blink his beady eyes just once. Then the pickup was upon him, turning his peaceful, *mañana* world into a roaring, stinking maelstrom.

The left-hand front tire clipped the edge of his tough shell, flipping him over and sending him skittering along in the vehicle's dusty wake.

A moment later the pickup was gone, leaving the tortoise to tumble and bounce several more feet before finally spinning to a lazy stop, balanced precariously on the tip of his green-brown carapace.

In seconds, his whole world had literally been turned upside-down.

His legs waved feebly in the muggy air. He turned his head one way, then the other, but could think of no way to turn himself right-side up again.

He was helpless.

How long he lay there, with the sun baking his vulnerable underside, he had no true grasp. But after about fifteen minutes, a shadow fell across him. Instantly, he withdrew his head, legs and stumpy tail.

A long-legged, lean-flanked man of about thirty studied him from behind dark grey Aviator sunglasses. Then he set his backpack and bedroll down and dropped to his haunches beside the tortoise.

'Nearly got you too, did he?' he muttered.

About thirty minutes earlier, Mitch Akins had come close to having his own world turned upside-down — permanently — when the red pickup had come speeding up the dirt road behind him.

His thoughts interrupted by the steadily

building growl of its engine, he'd looked back and seen the truck approaching fast. Hoping for a ride, he turned toward it and stuck out his thumb.

But the truck just kept coming. As it got closer and the driver made no attempt to slow down, Mitch got the craziest feeling that the vehicle was going to run him off the road.

Rather than wait to get splattered, he threw himself into a shallow, brush-choked gully, spilling his meagre possessions everywhere. He rolled over and over and landed in a clump of catclaw bushes. The spines scratched the hell out of him and ripped his blue denim shirt and jeans.

He wasn't a moment too soon.

The truck blasted on by, trailed by a rooster tail of dust. Mitch immediately sprang up and flipped the driver the bird. 'Crazy sonofabitch!' he yelled. The truck roared on, quickly vanishing in the sun-blurred distance, the driver not even bothering to check his rear-view mirror to review the results of his handiwork.

Dust and silence settled back over the desert. Still pissed, Mitch brushed himself off, but didn't really know why. He'd been on the road for a week now, and it showed. He needed a shave, a bath and a hot meal.

Especially a hot meal.

Now, pushing his sweat-stained baseball cap back off his curly black hair, he watched as the tortoise renewed his efforts to turn over. Without help, it was never going to happen.

A crude, well-weathered sign stood to one side of the road about twenty feet ahead. Mitch took off his Aviators and studied it briefly through pale blue eyes.

**SHELBY'S OASIS
GAS AND EATS
SEE PREHISTORIC DESERT
MONSTERS
AND WORLD'S BIGGEST
RATTLESNAKE!
3 MILES AHEAD!**

His belly grumbled. *Three miles*, he thought. Shit, he wasn't sure he had three miles left in him. He was already feeling shaky from hunger as it was, and the lack of food had pared his naturally-lean features down to the bone and given him a vaguely wolfish cast that was accentuated by his sharp, cleft chin.

He turned back to the tortoise and picked it up. It weighed about as much as a newborn baby. His stomach rumbled again. An idea occurred to him and he began to study the creature more speculatively.

'Wonder what you'd taste like, bud?'

There was only one way to find out.

Glancing around, he saw a pile of rocks about thirty yards away. Offering him shade, the rocks were sketched wine-red by the wispy flowers of spreading mesquitilla. It was the perfect place for a cookout.

Tucking the tortoise under his arm, he gathered up his gear and made his way through tangles of snakeweed and saltbush to reach the rocks. The tortoise struggled feebly in his grip. Mitch sensed he felt the deliberate, ponderous thump of its heart against his ribs.

'Don't think I can't do this,' he told it. He strode on, the tortoise remaining hidden in its shell.

On reaching the rocks, Mitch threw his gear down and looked around. Nearby was a jagged rock. Moving to it, he grasped the tortoise in both hands and raised it above his head.

The tortoise finally chanced a look out from beneath his shell. His eyes were black and moist, like wet coal.

'If you're hoping I got a soft spot for animals,' said Mitch, 'you'd better think again. 'Cause when a man's starving, he'll eat pretty much anything. And believe me, pal, I'm starving.'

Despite his tough talk inwardly he cringed at the idea of killing a tortoise. But like his old man always said: *Needs must when the Devil drives.*

Well, Old Nick was certainly driving him right then.

Do it, he told himself.

But before he could obey his own instruction, he thought again: *It weighs about as much as a newborn baby.*

He paused. Damn it. This was no time for sentiment.

Instead, he forced himself to be clinical about it. *It's no different than cracking an egg.*

Yeah, right.

Clenching his teeth, he braced himself and swung the tortoise down in one rapid motion. But at the last instant he couldn't do it and stopped short of making contact with the rock.

'Shit.'

He turned the tortoise over. From deep within its shell it studied him through cold, emotionless eyes.

'Damn you,' Mitch told it. He set it down. 'Get your sorry ass out of here before I change my mind.'

As if knowing that wasn't likely, the tortoise slowly extended its head, legs and tail and then plodded back toward the road, its mind already returning to thoughts of succulent teddy bear cholla.

★ ★ ★

It was only after the tortoise had gone on its way that Mitch got the damnedest feeling he was being watched.

Frowning, he looked around but saw no-one.

His surroundings just then were basic in the extreme: undulating dips and swells of hot white sand sprinkled with grey-green, green and yellow brush extending as far as the eye could see.

Here and there the landscape was broken by shaggy Joshua trees, spreading Palo Verde and bark-peeling juniper, the ever-present saguaro and organ pipe cactus and an occasional spill of car-sized rocks. In the far distance, seamed purple mountains stippled with yet more yellow brush formed a serrated buffer between land and sky. The sky itself was pale blue, near cloudless.

He wiped the sweat off his forehead, pulled his cap low over his eyes, snatched up his gear and followed the tortoise back to the road.

Two stifling hours later he came to another sign.

ANY MOMENT NOW!
SHELBY'S OASIS!
FOOD — GAS — SOUVENIRS
— SNAKES — SCORPIONS
— GILA MONSTERS!
500 YDS AHEAD!
DON'T MISS IT!

Just visible in the distance, and set well back from the dirt road, sat a tiny cluster of flat-roofed buildings. Removing his Aviators, Mitch studied the place and sighed. Any way you cut it, it looked like a dump. But it was the only dump around. And like his old man also used to say: *Beggars can't be choosers.*

As he put the Aviators back on he caught a sudden flash of movement out the corner of his eye, something dark, fleeting and surprisingly close.

Startled by its nearness and speed, he turned that way for a second look but saw only empty desert. Dismissing it as imagination, or maybe a trick of the heat, he started walking again.

By now it was late afternoon, and the westering sun was beginning to form long grey shadows to the east. The day had been oven-hot and windless. But now a breeze picked up, still stiflingly warm but better than nothing. It blew a couple of tumbleweeds toward him, and if he hadn't been so tired and hungry he would have dodged them. As it was, they caught against his shins, hampering his progress, and he had to kick them free before he could go any farther.

A third sign showed itself in the rich salmon-coloured glow of approaching dusk. It pointed to a side road leading to the clustered buildings. Beside the sign stood three weathered, sun-faded plywood camels and a palm tree.

THIS IS IT!
GO NO FARTHER!
SHELBY'S OASIS!
SEE DEADLY RATTLESNAKES,
GIANT SPIDERS AND DESERT
MONSTERS!

Mitch smiled without humour. *Go no farther!* He didn't intend to, at least not tonight. Instead, he made for a rocky outcrop thirty yards away, flopped down in shade, dragged his boots off and rubbed his blistered feet.

He was hot and thirsty, his whiskers itched and he felt as if he could sleep for a week. He would've, too, had he not been so goddamn hungry. But food was all he could think of now, and had been ever since his last skimpy meal.

When was that, anyway, he wondered. *Yesterday? Day before yesterday? Yeah, that sounded about right.* But to his belly, it seemed more like a lifetime ago.

Settling himself against a smooth rock, he tucked his Aviators into his shirt pocket, then pulled his cap over his eyes and tried to doze off.

All he could do now was wait for darkness.

Away to the west, the sun continued to bleed slowly into the mountains.

2

He dozed until the moon came up. Then he waked, yawned, and stretched the stiffness from his muscles. Dammit, he felt hungrier than ever. He had to eat, and soon. Grabbing one of his boots, he started to pull it on — then abruptly stopped as a thought struck him. Turning the boot upside-down he gave it a shake; as he did so a small, light brown object dropped into the sand at his feet — a bark scorpion.

'Jesus!'

He scrambled back out of its reach, then glanced skyward and thought sourly: *You and your fucking sense of humour.*

After he finished checking and stamping into his boots, he gathered his gear together and headed for the abandoned tourist trap.

From a distance, Shelby's Oasis had looked grim. Up close it looked even worse.

It consisted of three buildings, the first of which had once been a diner. A long, narrow, prefabricated building that was roughly the same size as a railroad car, it had a vestibule front and centre and a low, now-crumbling adobe wall built around its base.

It was in almost complete disrepair. Most of its windows had been broken, and when he chanced a look inside, the moonlight showed him that it had long-since been stripped of everything of value: its payphone, its stools, booths, Formica tables — even much of the pressed tin ceiling.

Disappointed, he moved on to the square, plank-built gas station beside it, which still retained some of its original white paint and red stripe. A green Bennett gas pump mottled with rust stood sentinel out front, and moonlight reflected dully off a flaking MINIMUM SERVICE sign that hung crookedly over the boarded-up door. A second sign, this one fixed at eye-level to the right of the door, urged customers to ASK FOR WOLF'S HEAD MOTOR OIL.

The roll-up door that led into the service bay had rusted in a half-open position. Mitch ducked under it, waited for his eyes to adjust to the deeper gloom and then looked around.

The bay reeked of grease and spilled gas. Dust greyed everything. A few rusted tools and an overturned Hastings filter box sat on a scratched workbench stained dark with oil. Empty oil cans had been stacked in one corner, and at some time in the past a two-post hydraulic car lift in the middle of the floor had been shut off in mid-air.

He picked his way to the open door in the rear wall. It led into a small, now-bare office with a locked back door.

He was just coming out again when he heard an insistent scratching sound coming from somewhere to his right.

' . . . the hell . . . ?'

Almost immediately, the scratching stopped.

He listened for a few seconds, wondering if this place really was as deserted as it looked.

Then —

Scra-scra-scratch.

Silence.

He frowned. As near as he could tell, the noise had come from over by the workbench.

Cautiously, he moved closer.

One step . . .

Two steps . . .

Three steps . . .

The second he reached the workbench the filter box suddenly flipped over and he came face to face with a huge, greasy-looking rat.

Startled, he reared back, and the rat, equally surprised, took off across the bench with a shrill squeak of alarm. It dropped down to the floor and blurred off into a shadowed corner, its claws beating a rapid tattoo against the oil-stained cement.

Releasing his breath, Mitch watched it go. For a moment longer his heartbeat continued to hammer in his ears. Then he took one final look around and decided there was nothing here for him.

He started back to the roll-up door, and was just ducking under the forks of the hydraulic lift to get there when, suddenly, they dropped.

He threw himself to one side an instant before they could crush him; and even as they hit the floor with a heavy metallic clang, he rolled over and slammed against the workbench with a thump that sent pain stabbing through his back.

Ignoring it, he leaped up, quickly felt behind him, closed one hand on a discarded wrench and prepared to defend himself.

The bay was quiet now but for the fading echoes the falling forks had made.

He sensed someone was in here with him. They had to be. And yet the longer he stood there, waiting for Christ knows what else to happen, the more he realised that he really *was* alone.

He glanced suspiciously at the car lift. Maybe the forks had just been waiting to drop, that the half-raised lift was an accident waiting to happen.

Maybe.

But in the very next moment he thought he heard the back door close softly and a key turn in the lock.

He ran back across the bay to the open office door. He peered cautiously inside, but the room was still empty, the back door, when he checked it, still locked tight.

He gripped the wrench tighter. *Had* someone else been in here? Or had he just misheard a perfectly natural night-sound and taken it for something else?

Retracing his steps, he noticed a basic switch-box on the wall to his right. He inspected it closely. It had two buttons, a green one marked with a thick black arrow pointing up and a red one marked with a thick black arrow pointing down.

It didn't take a genius to figure out that this was the control that worked the lift. He wondered if it was still connected, but decided against trying it. He'd already made enough noise as it was.

He ducked back outside, discarded the wrench and began walking down to the long, windowless structure that had once housed the snake-farm itself.

Every step of the way he had the creepiest feeling that he was being watched.

Forcing himself to concentrate on the business at hand, he gave the snake-farm a cursory inspection. It was little more than an elongated shack, though how it remained standing baffled him. The roof — what was left of it — sagged like a well-used hammock. There were gaping holes in the walls and the main door hung askew from one brittle hinge. He considered checking it out but decided it could wait.

Instead, he turned his back on the place and surveyed the surrounding desert, trying to decide his next move.

He didn't see a slim shadow move silently behind him.

It was dark save for the moon that occasionally came from behind the drifting clouds. By its light he saw that the dirt trail which had brought him to the snake-farm actually continued on over a brushy rise about fifty yards away. Curious, he decided to see where it led to.

When he crested the rise a few minutes later he stopped and gave a low whistle.

Below him the slope dropped toward a broad, brush-littered bowl of land at the centre of which, and completely hidden from the desert floor above, stood the last thing he'd been expecting to see.

A two-storey house.

It was a big, sprawling, asymmetrical kind of place, shingle-built and painted dark grey, with white casement window frames of every size and shape. Even in the poor light the place looked uglier than sin.

Eight wide steps led up to a porch, screen door and front door. To the left of the doors rose two four-window bays, one atop the other. To the right, the open porch curved around the house and out of sight. That side of the house, he saw, thrust out at an odd angle and had also been built in a curve. To accommodate the peculiar 'add-on' or 'afterthought' flavour of its architecture, the black-tiled roof seemed to be all pitch, point and turret.

It looked like a haunted house that was just waiting for the ghosts to move in.

It was also in complete darkness.

His hopes rising, he carefully descended the rock-littered slope and began checking the ground-floor windows. They were all locked. Undaunted, he worked his way around the house. But he found the storm doors and back door locked, too, and no other means of entry immediately apparent.

Then he got lucky.

More by chance than anything else, he noticed that the kitchen window at the side of the house had been left slightly open.

He snuck up to the window, listened for a moment, then put both hands on the frame and pushed upward. It lifted smoothly, noiselessly.

But before he could climb inside, he heard a faint sound behind him and quickly spun around to face it.

It was an odd kind of chirrup that ended with a distinct purring sound.

A second later he heard it again, somewhere out in the darkness: low, mournful and vaguely threatening.

Well, he thought, at least that explained the feeling he still couldn't seem to shuck: that he was being watched. But what kind of animal made *that* sort of noise?

Turning back to the house, he pulled

himself up onto the sill, threw his gear in ahead of him and then clambered carefully through the window and down off the kitchen sink. Once inside, he listened for a few moments to make sure he hadn't wakened anyone. When he was satisfied, he went to the fridge, opened the door and studied its contents.

Grinning, he helped himself to a plate of leftover chicken and began wolfing it down. God, he'd forgotten how good cold chicken could taste! He stuffed more into his mouth and chewed. The experience was almost sexual.

When he'd cleaned the plate, he took out a carton of milk and drained it. His hunger temporarily appeased, he wiped a sleeve across his mouth and stepped back —

— right onto a china pet bowl.

Shit!

It went skittering out from under him, spilling crunchy kibbles across the floor, making enough noise to wake the dead.

He froze, ears straining to catch any sound.

Silence.

Relaxing, he headed for the doorway. It led out into a musty, shadow-filled hallway and a wide flight of stairs. Everything about the place seemed to be old and run-down: the floral wallpaper was faded, the patterned carpets were thin and worn, the furniture was big, heavy and out of date.

He peered along the hallway. There were two doors in the facing wall, each one ajar. He crossed to the nearest and glanced inside. He realised then that both doors led into the same long room, some sort of den.

He went inside, looked around, saw a well-filled antique china cabinet, an equally old beech wood table upon which stood two brass candlesticks and a reading lamp, a well-stocked bar in the far corner, a Whitney upright piano and what appeared to be two large, stuffed armchairs and a sofa, covered in dust sheets.

Dominating the room was a wide stone fireplace. The old Napoleon hat-style clock on the mantel had stopped at 4:51 and, apparently, never been wound again.

Three framed photographs hung side by side over the cold hearth. The first showed a slim young girl smiling demurely at the camera with her white-gloved hands crossed over her flat stomach. She looked pale and slightly prim. Her dark, conservative dress covered her from the neck down to just below her knees. She wore small, tinted glasses and had her honey-blonde hair pulled back off her forehead and pinned in a bun. He guessed that she was about twenty.

The second photograph showed him a heavyset man in his late sixties, dressed in Levis, shirt and a sweat-stained Arizona Diamondbacks' baseball cap. His eyes were baggy, the expression on his shaggy-bearded face stern. He was leaning against an old red pickup truck, thick arms folded defiantly across his broad chest.

It was the third photograph, however, that really grabbed his interest.

It showed what he initially took to be the girl in the first picture, but now completely transformed. Now she looked wild, wanton, and a bold, predatory smile played across her full lips.

But this girl didn't wear glasses, and she wore her raven-dark hair in a crazy tousled and textured style. As for the sun-bronzed body . . . well, her cut-down Daisy Duke jeans and skimpy white top left little to the imagination. She knew what she had, this one, and he could see by her expression that she liked for everyone else to know it, too.

He could hardly believe it was the same girl, and when he leaned forward to take a closer look, getting so close that his breath actually fogged the glass, he saw that it wasn't. Quite apart from the obvious, the features of this little hellcat were ever-so-slightly different. Sisters? For sure. Twins, most likely. But as different as night and day.

He realised then that he'd been so intent on the picture that he'd allowed himself to become distracted from the business at hand.

Quickly, efficiently, he checked behind each picture in turn for a wall-safe, but found none. He spotted what appeared to be a square of newspaper pasted to the back of the picture of the old man, but paid it no mind.

Next he gave the rest of the room a careful onceover, checked beneath the dust sheets just in case they concealed anything worth stealing. When he still came up empty, he knew he'd have to try his luck upstairs.

He slipped out into the hall. Around him the house hissed with silence. He went to the staircase, set his weight down carefully on the first step, then took the second, third —

He was about halfway to the top when a floorboard creaked softly in the hallway below.

Nerves already stretched tight, he wheeled around fast, trapping the breath in his throat.

There came no further sound.

A long beat passed before he chanced another step, and then a new sound drew his attention to the head of the stairs: a faint, low growl.

No, he corrected himself, not a growl.

A chirrup that ended with a raspy purr.

He remembered the dish he'd kicked over, the same peculiar chirruping sound he'd heard outside, and allowed his jangled nerves to calm a little. It was a cat!

He started climbing again. He set his foot down on the next step, realised too late that it wasn't a step at all, it was something round and soft that had been left on the step, and lost his balance.

He made an urgent, panicky grab for the banister rail. He missed it and grasped thin air instead. And as he fell backward into the darkness, he could no longer stifle the urge to cry out.

He landed on his back, pain jagging along his spine and up into the back of his head. After that momentum and gravity did the rest, spilling him over, sideways and down, over, sideways and down, with a small, soft green ball — a cat's plaything — bouncing downwards ahead of him.

At last he flopped limply off the bottom stair and onto the hall floor, battered, beaten, unconscious.

3

When he came to, he was back in the den. He'd been dumped into a hard ladder-back chair and his hands had been tied — inexpertly, it felt — behind his back. His head was pounding, there was a persistent, nauseating throb in his lower spine and the room — which was now lit by two brass chandeliers overhead — seemed to be rotating slowly.

He felt stiff and ready to vomit, but a woman's voice nearby suddenly gave him something else to think about.

' . . . yes, sheriff, I *know* it's late, but you have to come and get this man! Diana and I are scared, and . . . yes, I *know* it's a long haul . . . '

He turned his head, wincing at the pain it caused in his stiff neck, and saw a woman on the other side of the room. Her back was to him and she had an old-fashioned black telephone pressed tight to her left ear. Although a decade must have passed since it was taken, he recognised her immediately from her photograph.

It was Miss Prim and Proper.

'But it's your *job* to protect us!' she said into the phone. Her voice was high, edgy, seemingly one breath away from a shriek. There followed a moment of silence, and then her shoulders sagged with relief. 'You *will?* Thank you, sheriff. Oh, and sheriff . . . ? Will you keep an eye out for Benjamin on your way over? He's been out all day, and you could easily run over him in the dark.'

As she hung up he tried to rise, but almost as soon as he put weight on his left leg he more or less collapsed again. He must've damaged his ankle in the fall, because he sure as fuck couldn't walk on it now. Silently cursing, he wondered if anything else was broken.

Hearing him drop back into the chair, Miss Prim and Proper turned quickly. In the harsh light she looked shockingly pale, the impression made even more so by the dark tint of her glasses. She still appeared to be slim, but it was hard to tell for sure because she was wrapped in a long old-fashioned pink robe.

She was also wearing white gloves, just the way she had been in the photo taken a decade earlier.

She took a steadying breath, said, 'Th-that was Sheriff Crane. He's on his way here to arrest you.'

'Why?' said Mitch. 'I haven't done anything.'

'You broke into my house to rob me.'

'I *didn't* rob you, though,' he reminded her.

'You would have, if you hadn't knocked yourself out first.'

She spoke in a sharp, clipped chatter, the voice of a woman who has always lived on her nerves.

'You're not the first burglar my sister and I have caught, you know. Like you, they believed all the rumours and thought they could get rich overnight.'

He frowned. 'Lady,' he said wearily, 'would you believe me if I told you I don't know what in hell you're talking about?'

He waited for a response that didn't come.

'I didn't think so.'

His attitude unsettled her, and she seemed to decide that the best way to fight her fear was to replace it with anger. 'You're greedy fools, all of you!' She knitted her gloved hands restlessly before her. 'Don't you understand? There *is* no gold! Papa never found the Lost Dutchman or any *other* legendary strike! When he died, the only gold he had was in his teeth!'

'Whoa! You think that's why I broke in here? To find your old man's gold?'

The green eyes behind her glasses slid away from his. 'What other reason could there be?'

She hurried out before he could answer.

'None that you'd believe!' he called after her. '*Your* mind's already made up!'

In the kitchen, she peeled the gloves from her hands and dropped them into the laundry hamper. Then she went to the fridge. Surprised to find the empty plate Mitch had left behind him, she took out a plastic bag containing several pairs of fresh white gloves.

Placing the bag on the sink, she quickly but thoroughly rinsed her hands under cold water.

'But I'll tell you this!' Mitch called from the den. 'You're gonna look pretty fucking stupid when your sheriff hears *my* side of it!'

Without drying her hands, she pulled on a fresh pair of gloves from the bag then put the remainder back into the fridge.

'What side's that?' she demanded, returning to the den.

'That I've been on the road for a week and I haven't slept or eaten in what seems like forever. I thought this place was empty and planned to crash here for the night. Turns out I was wrong, and I'm sorry. No harm, no foul.'

He could see that he was, if not exactly winning her over, at least planting a seed of doubt in her mind.

'Even if all that's true,' she hedged, 'which I doubt, it's still against the law to break into a person's home.'

'So? At worst I'm looking at a fine or a couple days in the can. No biggie.'

He moved his leg, grunting as pain ripped through his ankle and calf. Seeing him grimace, she asked uncertainly, 'Are you all right?'

'Like you give a shit.'

The accusation struck her like a calloused palm. 'Even thieves deserve consideration,' she said stiffly.

Realising that she really meant it, he lost some of his belligerence. 'I could use some water,' he said.

As she left to get him some, his teeth clamped hard and he went to work on the rope binding his wrists.

Shortly she returned with a glass of water. He watched her come and let her hold the rim to his whiskered lips. He took a few sips. The water was so cold that it almost stole his breath. Then he looked boldly into her face and chanced a brief smile.

'Thanks.'

Flustered by his smile and what she thought she'd seen in his eyes, she went to offer him another drink. When he brought his freed hands out from behind his back instead, she cried out and dropped the glass.

He lunged up out of the chair and tried to grab her. But he came down heavy on his injured ankle and promptly collapsed at her feet.

Keeping her distance, she watched him writhing on the floor. He gently massaged his leg. 'Aw, man, that hurts. Fucking thing must be broken!'

'Serves you right for trying to trick me. Now get back on that chair!'

He glared up at her, ready to chew nails and spit rust.

She snatched up one of the brass candlesticks. 'Do you want me to hurt you?'

He studied her. Unable to tell for certain whether or not she was bluffing, he slowly, gingerly dragged himself back up and flopped into the chair.

She moved around behind him, picked up the rope, said shakily, 'Let me have your hands.'

'Aw Jesus, give me a break, will you? You saw for yourself, I can't even *walk*, let alone attack you!'

She regarded him coolly. 'Hands.'

Mitch made no move to oblige her. 'What if I give you my word that I won't try to get away?'

The fine, arched brows above the glasses pinched together. 'Give me one good reason why I should trust you.'

''Cause I never break my word. *Never*. It's about the only thing I still got.'

She eyed him warily.

'Look, lady,' he said through clenched teeth, 'it's the middle of the night, I got no wheels, I can't walk and there's about a million fucking miles of desert out there. Even if I could get away, where the fuck would I go?'

His outburst brought a flush of colour to her alabaster cheeks. 'What's your name?'

'What's yours?'

'Agnes Shelby.'

Inwardly he smirked. *Agnes*. She sure *looked* like an Agnes. 'I'm Mitch,' he said. 'Mitch Akins.'

'Well, Mr Akins, if you want to go on talking to me, you'll moderate your language. I don't appreciate cussing.'

He fell silent.

'That ankle needs icing,' she said as he winced while trying to get comfortable.

Sensing that he might be winning her over at last, he said humbly, 'I'm sorry. For swearing, I mean. I got a big mouth and sometimes I don't know when to keep it shut.' He looked up at her, adding, 'Ice'd be great.'

Agnes left the room and took the rope with her. When she returned a few minutes later she was carrying a bowl filled with tinkling ice cubes. She set it down before him, knelt and began to untie his left boot-lace.

'So,' he said, 'what's with the gloves?'

She made a flustery, self-conscious little gesture. 'I have a skin allergy. I have to keep them covered. My doctor says I should really move somewhere cool and moist.'

'So why don't you?'

'I'm afraid this is going to hurt,' she said, easing the boot off. 'Oh, I'd leave in a heartbeat, but . . . '

She peeled off his sock and examined his puffy foot. A purple bruise, yellow at the edges, had already discoloured the ankle. Gently, she lowered his foot into the bowl. The feel of the ice made him suck air through clamped teeth.

'That feel better?'

'Lady,' he said, 'chopping my nuts off with a rusty axe would feel better than this.'

She smiled briefly. 'Would a brandy help?'

'Couldn't hurt.'

Rising, she went to the bar and poured a single glass of Korbels.

'You not joining me?'

'I only drink on . . . special occasions,' she said.

Mitch ran his eyes along the line of bottles on display. 'That's a lot of booze for someone who doesn't drink much.'

'My father drank,' said Agnes. She handed him the glass then threw back the dust sheet covering the sofa so that she could sit down. 'So does my sister.'

Mitch gestured to the pictures over the fireplace. 'She's a hottie.'

'I'm sorry?'

'A hottie,' he repeated. 'You know, sexy. Great body. Buns to die for.' He took another look at the photograph, adding, 'In a wild kind of way.'

Agnes studied the photograph, her expression wistful. 'Oh yes,' she murmured. 'Diana's wild, all right. Always was.'

'And you?' prodded Mitch. 'I bet you were always the quiet one, huh?'

She gave an embarrassed, almost apologetic half-shrug.

'Well, you know what they say about still waters running deep.' When he saw her cheeks flush he added, 'Don't be embarrassed. I meant it as a compliment.'

When she still didn't reply, he said, 'Is that why you didn't move? Because of your sister?'

'Diana loves the desert,' she said by way of answer. 'It's like her, I suppose. Wild. Free. She says she'd die if we ever moved to a city.'

'So you suck it up, itch and wear gloves?'

'It's a small price to pay to keep someone you love happy.'

'I wouldn't know,' said Mitch, draining his glass. 'I've never loved anyone.' He

38

glanced around. 'Where is she now?'

'Out there somewhere.' Agnes gazed sadly at the four-window bay and the desert night beyond. ' 'Living free,' she calls it. Sometimes she's gone for days.'

'Doesn't it worry you?'

His foot began to ache with the cold, and he carefully lifted it from the bowl. In an instant Agnes was back on her knees before him, wrapping his foot in a towel and gently patting it dry.

'I mean, what if she broke a leg or . . . I don't know . . . got bitten by a snake. Shit happens, you know.'

'Oh, I know, all right.' She gently slipped the sock back over his foot and then held his boot as he put it back on. 'And yes, I do worry. But she just laughs, says the desert and all its creatures are her friends. She says she's safer out there than anywh — '

She broke off suddenly and canted her head, bird-like.

'What is it?' asked Mitch.

'Rats,' hissed Agnes. 'Gnawing. Don't you hear them?'

Without waiting for a reply, she got up

and crossed to the wall beside the door. Putting her ear to the plaster, she said in a low, tight voice, 'I hear you, rats! Don't think that I don't!'

She continued, almost to herself, 'They live inside the walls, you know. I hear them at night. Sometimes their gnawing gets so loud it keeps me awake.'

Mitch watched her return to the sofa, once again fidgeting nervously with her hands. He hoped she couldn't tell what he was thinking from his expression. He tried to think of something to say, but her odd behaviour had been a conversation-stopper. The best he could come up with was, 'Lucky you got a cat.'

Her whole manner seemed to undergo a sudden softening. 'Yes,' she said. 'Dear, sweet Benji. If it weren't for him, we'd be overrun with vermin.'

Mention of the cat distracted her, and without another word she got up and left the room. Mitch tensed, listening to the sounds she made heading for the front door. He heard the door open, then Agnes calling peevishly, 'Benji, where are you?'

He knew then that he was never going to get a better chance to get out of there.

'Benji? Do you hear me? Come on . . . '

He got up, trying to keep his weight off his injured ankle, and hobbled to the door nearest to the kitchen. Peering around the frame, he saw Agnes standing just inside the front doorway, staring out into the night.

'*Benjamin!*' she called, her voice suddenly hardening. 'I'm *calling* you, you bad boy!'

Snatching up his back pack and bedroll, he shuffled across the hallway, into the kitchen. Ignoring the window by which he'd first entered, he went directly to the back door.

It was locked.

'Benji . . . '

Dammit!

He scanned the kitchen, knowing he didn't have much time. Quickly he checked the drawers, ran his palms across the counter.

*Shit . . . *

'Benji-i-i . . . '

Fresh out of ideas, he opened the

broom closet door. Hanging on a hook was a key and he felt a sudden surge of triumph. He snatched the key, grabbed a mop as an afterthought, and using it as a makeshift crutch, fumbled his way to the door.

'Benji!'

Ignoring Agnes, he tried the key in the lock. It fitted! He unlocked the door, eased it open and hobbled out into the night.

He knew he couldn't go far. He tried to favour his ankle but it felt like hell, and every step seemed to tear a little bit more life out of him.

After forty yards he had to stop. He half-fell against a rock, sweating hard and gasping like a rain-filled accordion. He looked back at the house, but thankfully saw no sign of Agnes.

Although it was the last thing he wanted to do right then, he forced himself to push on, hopping, shuffling, moving any way he could to keep putting distance between himself and the woman who'd called the cops on him.

He made it about halfway up the rise

before the mop-handle broke. It snapped with a sound like a gunshot and he sprawled face-first onto the ground.

'Fuck!'

The curse was torn from him, but he knew he couldn't afford the luxury of self-pity right then. He had to keep moving.

Discarding the short end of the mop handle, he crawled into the cover of some rocks. Here he rolled onto his back and sucked greedily at the cold night air.

That was when he heard it.

Chirruping.

He froze, then slowly sat up on one elbow and peered out into the darkness to his left. For the space of half a dozen heartbeats there was nothing but the background hiss and rattle of cicadas.

Then —

It came again, much closer this time and from somewhere off to his right. It ended again in a raspy purr that sounded menacing. Mitch turned that way, flinching at the pain in his leg.

Get a grip, he told himself irritably. *It's a cat, for chrissake, not a fucking tiger.*

And yet there was something in that low, persistent chirrup that was not plaintive or appealing, but —

It came again, louder, closer, somewhere off to his right again. And this time it sounded definitely threatening.

Unable to shake the idea that the cat was somehow stalking him, he used the broken mop handle to help him struggle back to his feet and hobble on. He needed someplace to hole up until after the sheriff had come and gone; someplace to rest his ankle until daylight.

Somehow he made it to the ridge, glancing around warily every laboured step of the way. Fifty yards ahead he spotted the silhouette of the snake-farm and again he thought, *Beggars can't be choosers.*

He stumbled toward the dilapidated building. The mournful yipping cry of a distant coyote broke the silence. It was a familiar sound yet for some unknown reason it made him look nervously about him.

Then, at last, he was there.

He hauled the sagging door open and

limped into a sticky curtain of old spider-webs. Swearing, he clawed them away from his face and looked around the room, which was illuminated dully by what little moonlight fell in through the holes in the roof.

Glass cases lined the walls on either side of him. Shuffling between them by way of a narrow central aisle, Mitch made out the shadowy shapes of long, coiled rattlesnakes, fat Gila monsters, thick-legged spiders and glossy scorpions.

They were all dead.

'Jesus . . . '

Maybe this wasn't such a good place to hole up in after —

Something dark fell from a rafter above him, and instinctively he moved to catch it.

Big mistake.

It was a large black tarantula with dark stiff hair, bigger than his outspread hand.

Even though it was dead, just like everything else in this glorified mausoleum, it filled him with revulsion. He gasped and flung it off into the darkness at the far end of the shack.

Outside the door, he heard a soft *chirrup*.

He spun around, his temper flaring again. *Come on then, Benji. Come on in and I'll wring your freaking neck.*

But for all his bravado, he realised that he was backing away from the door, using the glass cases for support and holding the broken mop handle before him like a weapon.

The chirruping came again. It had a whiny, petulant tone, as if the cat hated to be cheated of its prey.

Tough, he thought.

For the next minute or so his attention remained fixed on the door. But when the silence stretched on and there were no more sounds, he finally realised that the cat was gone.

He sagged with relief.

In the distance the coyote howled again, and releasing a long-held breath, he hobbled back to the door and listened at one of the rotted panels.

Nothing.

Right. Whether he liked it or not, then, he had to get back on the move, because he sure as hell wasn't spending the night in here.

Stepping back outside, he hop-shuffled to the corner of the building, telling himself that it was going to take forever to get off this damn' desert. Just then he heard a soft sound behind him.

He turned, half-expecting to see the cat arching its back and getting set to start spitting.

Instead a figure detached itself from the darkness, a figure in a sexy yellow halter top and Daisy Duke cut-offs, and he thought: *Diana*.

Then she stepped into the moonlight, and to his surprise he saw that she had streaked her tanned face with white Apache war paint.

Before he could say anything she raised the two-by-four she'd been holding like a club and struck him hard alongside the head.

Pain exploded in his left ear and he stumbled sideways. Balance shot to hell, he fell to his knees, and before he could recover, her moon-thrown shadow dropped over him like a shroud.

He looked up at her through glazed eyes, saw that painted face again, surrounded by a wild tangle of blue-black hair. She seemed to snarl, and when she did, her green eyes came to life, opened wide and turned feral.

She clubbed him again, and the world around him went very, very black.

4

The moment he regained consciousness he tried to sit up, but the throbbing in his head made him dizzy so he remained where he was.

Taking care to keep his movements to a minimum, he slowly inspected his surroundings. He was stretched out on a soft bed in a good-sized room decorated with dull floral wallpaper and chunky furniture. Someone had put his back pack, bedroll and baseball cap on a ladder-back chair beside the dressing-table.

He closed his eyes again, hurting too much to really care where he was. One thing was certain, though — unless they'd hired Norman Rockwell to refurbish their cells, he hadn't yet been dragged off to the county jail.

Sensing another presence nearby, he reopened his eyes and saw Agnes in the doorway, arms folded, watching him with an expression he was unable to read.

He said in a tired, scratchy voice, 'Seems all I do around you is get beat up.'

'You gave me your word you wouldn't try to escape,' she said crossly.

'So I lied. Sorry.' He glanced around the room. 'You carry me all the way up here by yourself?'

She gave him the fluttery, flustery gesture that was rapidly becoming her trademark. 'Diana helped me. She's also the one who hit you.'

That triggered a brief flash of memory: of wild green eyes in a white-striped face, and tangled hair accentuating the craziness he saw just before she clobbered him the second time.

'She said to tell you she was sorry for hitting you so hard,' Agnes went on.

Mitch snorted. 'I'm sure it broke her heart. What do you guys call yourselves, anyway — the Concussion Sisters?'

'Sarcasm is the lowest form of wit.'

She came deeper into the room. 'While you were unconscious, we went through your things.'

'You *what?*'

'We didn't steal anything.'

'That's 'cause I got nothing *worth* stealing.'

'Your driver's licence has expired.'

'How about that?' he replied bitterly. 'Can you believe those assholes at the Tucson DMV? They actually wanted me to *pay* for the renewal.'

'Is that why you've been walking? Because you couldn't afford to renew your licence?'

She seemed to be looking for a reason to understand him, or maybe to pity him. Either way, he wasn't about to oblige her.

'Let me see now,' he mused. 'Was it that, or was it because those repo pricks snatched my truck last week?'

She grew irked. 'Are you always this charming?'

'Pretty much.'

'Why didn't you just go out and get a job?'

'I'll tell you why,' he said, as if addressing a small child or a village idiot. 'I'm a trucker, see, and the folks who *hire* truckers have this crazy notion that their drivers ought to have *licences*. Which kind of puts me between a rock and a hard place.'

'Meaning that you can't afford the licence until you get a job? And you can't get a job until you've got the licence, is that it?'

'You got it.'

'So what if . . . '

'What?'

'Nothing.'

'Go on, spit it out.'

She said hesitantly, 'What if I could *help* you?'

'Lady, you've already done enough just by calling the sheriff.'

Waving that aside with one gloved hand, she said, 'I mean, if I knew of a way you could make . . . say, five hundred dollars?'

'Sounds great. Who do you want me to kill?'

'No-one. And I . . . I'd be willing to forget that you broke into my house as well.'

'So what's the catch?'

'There isn't one.'

'Listen, Agnes, there's *always* a catch. So what exactly do you want from me?'

Again she hesitated before saying softly, 'A . . . favour.'

'Let me guess,' he said. 'You and Baby Jane want to play stickball with my head.'

'My God, you're cynical.'

'You can blame that on my not-so-privileged childhood. Just one of the many unpleasant side-effects of growing up around a couple of full-time drunks.'

Although he couldn't see her eyes behind the glasses, he saw her brows lower and figured she was feeling a tinge of compassion.

'I . . . I'm sorry,' she said softly. 'I've obviously misjudged you. I thought that beneath all that bravado there was — '

' — a nice guy trying to get out?' he finished. 'Sorry to disappoint you, Agnes, but I'm all out of nice.'

'So it appears. Diana was right — as always. I was stupid to even *consider* the idea. I can see now that it never would've worked.'

'What wouldn't have worked?'

Agnes left the room. A moment later he heard her washing her hands again in a bathroom across the hall. Carefully, Mitch sat up and swung his legs over the edge of the mattress. The world tilted unpleasantly, and he hurriedly swallowed bile.

'Look, I'm sorry I've disappointed you,' he called out. 'I disappoint myself all the time.'

The water stopped running and he listened to the heavy silence that followed it.

'Just humour me, okay? Tell me what your idea was.'

Nothing.

'I know I'm going to jail, but I'd still like to know what I missed out on.'

Silence continued to fill the house. Shortly Agnes reappeared in the doorway, adjusting the fit of a fresh pair of white gloves.

'I wanted you to . . . oh God, it sounds crazy when I think about it. But I wanted you to pretend to be . . . my fiancé.'

Mitch narrowed his eyes. 'You better say that again. For a minute there I thought you said fiance.'

Agnes took an impulsive step closer to him, her fingers knitting and fidgeting before her. 'It'd just be for three days,' she went on in a rush. 'That's why . . . why I

54

thought we might pull it off.'

Mitch eyed her thoughtfully. 'You're serious about this, aren't you? Jeez. Why would you want to pull a stunt like that?'

'Tomorrow, my brother Scott and his new wife are coming to spend the weekend. While they're here, I want them to . . . to think we're engaged.'

'Why?'

'That's my business.'

'Okay,' he allowed. 'We'll skip that for now. But what about Diana? Will *she* go along with it?'

'Diana will do whatever I tell her.'

'And the sheriff? He's expecting to find a burglar, remember.'

'I'll handle Sheriff Crane,' she assured him.

It sounded crazy, he thought, though no crazier than anything else that had happened to him tonight. Besides, he didn't really have much choice in the matter, not if he wanted to keep his freedom.

'All right,' he said finally. 'Count me in. But you'll have to give me a crash-course on yourself.'

'All right.'

'And . . . '

'Yes?'

Their eyes met, his beginning to clear at last, hers, behind the dark glasses, still largely a mystery to him.

'I'll want the money up front,' he said.

'Half now, half when they leave.'

He grinned. 'Deal.'

The word had barely left his lips when yellow headlights swept across the window, accompanied by the sounds of a car engine and tires turning against hardpan.

Mitch stiffened. 'The sheriff?'

Agnes went to the window, brushed the curtain aside. He watched her reflection in the night-dark glass.

'Yes.' She turned back to him. 'You clean up while I go talk to him.' At the door she stopped briefly. 'Oh, and if you look in the closet over there, you'll find an old pair of crutches. They used to belong to Papa.'

* * *

As he brought his Chevy Tahoe to a halt and killed the engine, Mel Crane studied the Shelby place through his dusty windshield and thought, not for the first time, that it was a dismal, desperate dump in which to waste one's life.

'Course, he could understand it of Agnes Shelby. For as long as he'd known her she'd always been scared of her own shadow, so she probably found the solitude to her liking. But Diana . . . well, he'd never quite figured out why a live-wire like her had settled for a life out here, a life that was really no life at all.

With a weary sigh he picked up his immaculate pearl-grey Stetson, climbed out of the car and closed the door. Then he set the hat carefully, almost lovingly atop his balding head and went up the steps to the front door.

He was a tall man in his late fifties. He had a tough, waxy face and sad, close-set eyes the colour of dark chocolate, and though he was starting to thicken around the waist now that he was reaching the end of his long career in law enforcement, he still managed to cut an imposing figure in his well-tailored coffee-brown suit, white shirt and steer's-head bolo tie.

Crane was a veteran cop with close to forty years' experience in almost every aspect of police work. Intelligent, intuitive and determined, he also held an A.Sc in Law Enforcement, a B.A. in Criminal Justice and a B.Sc in Public Administration and Criminal Justice Management.

These days, however, it was said by many — though *never* to his face — that he was just a guy going through the motions.

There was a reason for that and it was a good one. But Crane saw no point in going over it again, even though it seemed to him that he went over it a million times a day whether he wanted to or not.

In any case, right now he had a job to do. He'd been called out to Shelby's Oasis to arrest a burglar, only to discover, as Agnes Shelby showed him nervously into the den, that the burglar had somehow managed to escape her custody.

'We were only in the kitchen for fifteen minutes,' she explained breathlessly. 'Just long enough to heat up the coffee. Oh, that reminds me. Would you like a cup, sheriff?'

Trying not to show his irritation at being called out on what amounted to a fool's errand, Crane thanked her and said yes.

'Cream and sugar?'

'Black.'

He watched her leave, then almost reverently set his beloved Stetson on the coffee table and took out his notebook and pencil.

It was said that the Stetson was Crane's pride and joy, and it was equally true to say that he guarded it with his life.

'Here you go,' said Agnes, re-entering the room. 'Be careful, it's hot.'

She put the cup down next to the Stetson, and he quickly moved the hat out of harm's way.

'Thank you ma'am.' He perched on the edge of a now-uncovered armchair. 'So, let me get this straight. You say you were in bed when you heard some kind of disturbance down here. And when you and Diana came to investigate, you found a man about to ransack the drawers in that cabinet over there?'

'Yes. It was a terrible shock. Terrible.

Luckily, Diana had thought to bring Papa's .45 down with her, otherwise I dread to think what might have happened.'

'So you caught this feller before he could really get started?'

'Yes.'

'Well, that's something, at least. What did he look like?'

She pretended to think about it. 'He was short, a little below average height. Stocky. Fair hair, about collar-length. A round face, clean-shaven. No real, ah, distinguishing features.'

'Age?'

'Early to mid-twenties.'

'What was he wearing?'

'Jeans. Some sort of grey sweater, a black leather jacket.'

He wrote that down. 'So what happened?'

Again she paused, as if recalling the events of the evening. 'Diana told him to put his hands up which he did. Then we told him to sit in that chair and I tied his hands, then called you.'

'So while you and Diana were in the

kitchen, the perp was tied to this chair here?'

Agnes nodded. 'Well, he wasn't tied *to* it. I tied his hands behind his back.'

'And when you returned, he was gone?'

'Yes. I, uh, guess I didn't tie him as well as I thought.'

'So how do you think he escaped? Out the window there? Through the front door?'

'Well, it couldn't have been the window, because it's been stuck fast since before Papa died.'

'The front door, then? Was that open?'

'I can't remember. Maybe. Diana's the one who discovered he was gone and she ran out after him.'

'And she's off in the desert now?'

'Yes. I begged her to stay until you got here, but you know Diana. Once she makes her mind up about something . . . '

Crane glanced around the den. 'What about your hired man? What's his name again?'

'Neon.'

'Where was *he* all this time?'

'In town. Sometimes he spends the

night there.' Frowning suddenly, she said, 'By the way, did you see Benji when you drove up? He still hasn't come home, the bad boy.'

Crane shook his head, checked his notes again. 'Did the perp have a car, do you know?'

Agnes made her familiar fluttery gesture. 'I don't think so . . . Everything happened so fast and . . . '

'No matter,' he cut in. He sipped his coffee. 'But you say that your boyfriend — '

'Fiancé,' she corrected. 'Mitch and I are engaged.'

'Congratulations. You say that your fiance arrived shortly after the perp escaped, yes?'

Agnes fidgeted. 'I believe I said burglar, not perp.'

Ignoring that, Crane said, 'I'd like to have a few words with him, if that's okay.'

Agnes's eyebrows arched. 'What for? *He* didn't see anything.'

'I'd still like to talk to him. When I drove up here, I didn't see any other cars around, so as much as anything else, I'd like to know how he got out here.'

'Oh, that's easy. He drove Papa's truck. You didn't see it because it's parked up behind the diner, under a tarp.'

'Well,' Sheriff Crane said politely but firmly, 'I'd still appreciate a few words.'

'Of course. I'll, uh . . . fetch him . . . '

Mitch was already trying to negotiate the stairs with his new-found crutch tucked under his arm. He'd shaved hurriedly and changed clothes, and no longer resembled the trail-weary vagabond who'd invaded Agnes's life earlier that evening.

'Oh, there you are, sweetheart.' Agnes stepped out into the hallway. 'I was just coming to get you.'

Mitch, who'd been listening to the conversation from the head of the stairs, finally made it to the bottom step, where he allowed Agnes to take his free arm and lead him into the den. Crane, surprised to see Agnes' fiancé injured, stood up and extended his hand.

Agnes introduced them. They shook hands and Crane said, 'Here, let me help you, son.'

As the sheriff guided him to the couch, Mitch asked, 'Have you caught the guy yet?'

'Uh-uh. But we're on it.'

He sat at the other end of the couch and gestured to Mitch's foot. 'Nasty-looking ankle you're nursing there, Mr Akins. What happened?'

'It's all my fault,' Agnes said quickly. 'If I'd tidied up the way I should have . . . '

Following her lead, Mitch said, 'I don't blame you, honey. I blame that dumb cat.' To Crane he explained, 'Benji left a ball about halfway up the stairs. I trod on it and next thing I know, I'm sprawled out on the hallway floor and Agnes is all over me like Mother Teresa.'

'Nothing broken, I hope?'

'I twisted it, is all.' Mitch nodded at the immaculate Stetson. 'Cool hat.'

'Gift from my wife,' Crane said, proudly and sadly. ''Fore she passed on.'

'Looks brand new.'

'Mabel liked things that way. She always took pride in a neat appearance.' He sighed, adding, 'Where you from, Mr Akins?'

'Tucson. Before that, Sedona. Where we met, right, honey?'

'I was there looking at the local art,' said Agnes.

'That what you are, then, Mr Akins? An artist?'

'I *wish*,' Mitch said with feeling. 'Trucker. Had my own rig, till the transmission went south.'

Seeing the sheriff's frown, he continued easily, 'You're wondering about the connection, right? A lot of people do. But it's simple. I was hauling a load out of Prescott when I blew a tire. I went into this coffee shop while it was being fixed and there was Agnes, looking just like an angel.'

Agnes simpered with feigned embarrassment. 'It was love at first sight, as they say. And we've been together ever since.'

'Well, I wish you a long and happy marriage,' Crane said. 'It's a wonderful institution, son.'

Mitch grinned. 'Sure. But who wants to live in an institution, right?'

Crane smiled politely. 'I don't suppose you happened to see anything of this burglar by any chance, Mr Akins?'

''Fraid not. He was long gone by the time I got here.'

The sheriff flipped his notebook shut and got to his feet, then bent and picked up his beloved hat, automatically brushing an imaginary speck of dust off its curled brim.

'Well, that's it, I reckon. For the time being, at least.'

'I'm only sorry you had a wasted journey,' Agnes said.

Not taking his eyes off Mitch, Crane said, 'Oh, I wouldn't say it was wasted. I got to meet your, uh, fiancé, here, didn't I?'

Agnes had to fight hard to keep her smile from slipping. 'Well, yes. There is that to it.'

'Your burglar was probably just an opportunist who bit off more than he could chew. He's probably long gone by now, as Mr Akins here says, but I'll put out an A.P.B. just in case, and we'll see what that turns up.'

'Thank you, sheriff.'

He nodded. 'I'll see myself out.'

As he brushed past her, she turned to Mitch. Both of them were holding their breath. Only when the door closed behind the sheriff did they expel sighs of relief; and when they heard him gun his engine and drive away, they exchanged grins.

'You know something, honey?' said Mitch.

'What, sweetheart?'

'We make a pretty good team, you and me.'

5

Diana lay back on the hood of the truck parked behind the diner and gazed up at the moon. The night was well advanced, and a cool wind ruffled her raven hair and made her nipples stiffen and push against the thin fabric of her halter top. It was a pleasant sensation.

Off in the distance, a coyote yip-yipped. It was one of the few desert sounds she despised; it seemed to carry with it all the loneliness and longing in the world, and loneliness and longing were two emotions she knew only too well.

After a time she slipped down off the truck and padded restlessly through the night until she reached the ridge overlooking the silent house.

Agnes's new man was down there.

Agnes's fiancé.

The thought made her smile coolly. Moonlight glistened on her fine white teeth.

Somewhere behind her the coyote howled again. She tilted her head and listened to it.

Loneliness, she thought.

Longing.

At last she moved.

She slunk down the slope toward the house, her movements silent and supple, her strong shoulders held well back, her hips thrust well forward, her long, slim legs working seductively with every nimble step she took.

Loneliness and longing.

She knew of only one way to keep them at bay.

★   ★   ★

It had been a long day, and Mitch was asleep almost the moment his head hit the pillow.

His sleep was deep and dreamless. He didn't even stir when his bedroom door opened and then closed again, near-silently, a few seconds later.

Diana's shadow slithered across him.

Standing beside the bed, she looked

down at him with a mixture of curiosity and hunger. Glittering green eyes traced the shape of his sheet-covered body, the curve of his muscular biceps, the broad swell of his chest, the shadowed bulge of his crotch, the long, lean lines of his legs.

She liked what she saw.

At length she set her weight gently on the edge of the bed.

He jerked awake then — and promptly froze, his eyes going wide.

For Diana was holding the blade of a long, sharp hunting knife against his throat.

Heart hammering, he swallowed, felt the weight of the keen blade press insistently against his Adam's apple and then did his best to stop breathing.

In the dark he could see only her silhouette: slim, sleek, sexy, her oval face — tanned deep bronze but wiped clean of war-paint now — surrounded by a wild snarl of midnight-black hair. She was breathing softly: he felt each gentle exhalation caress the side of his face. She smelled of sage and creosote, of desert star and ghost flowers: of the outdoors: of the desert.

'Wha — ?'

She put a finger to her lips to indicate silence. With the knife at his throat, he needed no second urging.

Then she brought her face down to his, and he felt the heat radiating from her. She touched her heart-shaped lips to his: they were soft and warm, and despite the knife he responded, kissing back, opening his mouth, tasting her tongue with his.

Some incalculable time later she drew back slowly, both of them breathing harder now. He opened his mouth, began to whisper a question —

A low, hissing chirrup filled the room.

Diana turned to the window. Mitch did the same.

There, on the sill of the open window, stood a big, slate-grey cat, his back arched, his pale copper-coloured eyes bright and hateful, his tiny mouth yanked wide in a snarl.

Benji.

Before Mitch could say anything, Diana hurled the knife at the cat.

The blade thunked into the frame just inches from Benji's front paws. He arched his back even higher, spat again, then whirled around and leaped into darkness.

Wordlessly she got up, appearing part feline herself, went over and pulled the knife out of the woodwork, then returned to the bed. Mitch tensed, not sure what she was going to do next, and muttered, 'You're pretty handy with that thing.'

She held the blade to his lips. It was cold and sharp and it delivered her message to perfection.

Shut up.

Then she set the knife on the bedside table, curled her fingers under the hem of her top and pulled it off over her head.

He swallowed hard.

She dropped the garment at her feet, unbuttoned her cut-offs and then slowly, deliberately drew down the zipper.

It made a soft purring sound in the silence.

The shorts dropped to her ankles and she stepped out of them.

She wasn't wearing panties.

Watching her, his lust growing stronger

in the pit of his belly, Mitch studied her like a man in a trance.

By any standard, she was stunning. Her long neck curved down to strong, wide shoulders. Her apple-sized breasts stood high and firm, each one crowned by a dark, erect nipple. She tapered at the waist, flared again at the hips, and as he allowed his eyes to roam across her flat stomach and then on down to the curly web of hair between her legs, he felt a little light-headed.

Still without speaking, she pulled the sheet back, exposing him. Then she climbed on top of him, reached down, closed her fingers around his hardness and slowly, expertly, guided him into her. She moaned, a soft, grateful sound, and began to grind, slowly at first, then with ever-increasing momentum.

In those first few seconds it was all Mitch could do to hold back. But then, as her passion gripped him, he brought his hands around to cradle her butt, and began to rise to meet her every downward plunge.

Sensing in some nameless way that she

wanted this to be rough and animalistic, he dug his fingers hard into her flesh and began to force her up and down on his manhood, fast, then faster, and she went along willingly.

In those next frantic, feverish moments, nothing else mattered — not Agnes, not the situation into which he'd stumbled, not the need to be quiet or discreet, *nothing*. He was completely consumed by her, by what they were doing, by the fact that this had nothing to do with love nor even affection, but a pure, animal need for the most basic form of satisfaction.

Roughly he threw her onto her back, knowing by her low, appreciative whine that it was exactly what she wanted. He rolled on top of her, pinning her with his weight, then plunged back into her and thrust hard and fast, again, again, again, his hips now an almost brutal, pumping blur.

She brought her legs up and around, crossed her ankles in the small of his back; and still he pushed and drove and plunged, gasping into her right ear, some small, distant part of him taking pleasure from the grunts and mewling sounds she made in return.

And then she went stiff, arched her back beneath him, dug her fingernails into the meat of his shoulders and nipped at his throat, and with one great shudder he emptied himself into her. And in that moment he knew *she* was the best ever, that *it* was the best ever.

And this, he told himself distantly, from a woman who, earlier, had knocked him unconscious.

★ ★ ★

Afterwards she lay in his arms and stared silently into the darkness. He didn't quite know what to say.

Thanks?

Oh, by the way, my name's Mitch, I'm your sister's fake fiancé?

In any case, he sensed that she was in no mood for conversation.

Somewhere out in the night, the coyote howled again. Or maybe it was a different coyote. Either way, it made Diana stir restlessly, rise up from the crumpled, sex-smelling sheets and begin to dress.

Mitch broke his silence at last. 'Wait.'

She turned to him, shadows dappling her body like spills of ink.

'Don't go,' he whispered.

'I have to.'

'Why?'

Diana glared balefully at the door. 'Agnes,' she hissed. 'You don't how jealous she can be. If she saw me here, if she saw us . . . I don't know what she'd do.'

Before he could respond, she bent, kissed him softly on the lips, then ghosted to the door and let herself out.

Mitch reached up and touched his mouth. After she'd gone he felt very, very lonely.

⋆ ⋆ ⋆

The following morning, he hobbled downstairs to a breakfast of Portuguese sausage, bacon, toast, pancakes, omelettes and fresh-squeezed orange juice. Agnes, dressed in a drab, high-necked grey dress, and as usual wearing her white gloves and tinted glasses, hummed softly as she set his plate before him. She seemed oddly energised, he thought, as if she'd started to enjoy the fantasy of being one half of a happy couple.

'Man, this looks great,' he said, digging in.

'Papa used to say that I made the best omelettes this side of the Grand Canyon. I'd ask, 'What about the other side?' and he'd say, 'Nothin' but Republicans on the other side, Princess,' and he'd laugh . . . '

Quite suddenly she fell into a reflective mood. 'I don't know why he thought that was so funny. But he did, and I was just happy because *he* was happy.'

'Sounds like you guys had fun together.'

She came and sat across from him, some of her animation returning. 'We did. Lots. I was Papa's favourite. Everyone knew that.'

'I bet that went over big with Diana and Scott.'

'Oh, they didn't care. They had Momma. She spoiled them rotten — that's why they were so devastated when she died, especially Scott. He cried himself to sleep for weeks afterward.'

Recalling the events of the previous night, Mitch asked casually, 'And Diana? How did she take it?'

Agnes gave him her trademark fidgety shrug. The kitchen was filled with sunshine, and the hard light made her skin look paler than bleached flour.

'That's when she started roaming the desert. Papa and I should have reined her in, I suppose, but we had bigger problems right then.'

'Oh?'

'They were building the new interstate. It was supposed to follow the old road, but the Highway Commission changed their minds at the last minute and moved it three miles away. Gradually people stopped coming out here and, well, business dried up.'

'Must've been tough. How'd you get by?'

'Momma left us kids a little cash. And Papa got a job down at the County Clerk's office in Tucson.'

He stopped chewing and frowned at her. 'I thought he was a prospector?'

'Only on weekends,' she said. 'But after a few months, something happened. I don't know what. But he quit working and started prospecting full-time. That's about when the rumours started flying . . . '

'About him finding the Lost Dutchman?'

She nodded. 'One of the clerks said that Papa had told him he'd found a record of the original claim.'

'But you didn't believe him?'

'Of course not. Papa would have told me if he'd found anything. And even if he hadn't, how could he bury a fortune in gold around here without my knowing? The whole thing's absurd — but you can't convince my stupid brother of that. Ever since Papa died and left the Oasis to me, Scott's been dying to dig the place up.'

Seeing that he was finished, she rose and took his empty plate to the sink. 'That's why he's coming here this weekend,' she continued. 'He says it's because he wants me to meet his new wife, but I know better. He's like King

Midas. His whole world revolves around greed.'

Mitch got up, favouring his leg, and joined her at the sink. Grabbing a towel, he started drying cutlery.

'But if there really *is* gold around here, don't you want to find it?'

'That's not the issue,' she snapped. 'There isn't any, and even if there was, I wouldn't want my privacy ruined by a mob of gold-crazy excavators.'

'Okay, okay,' he said. 'Don't have a cow. I get it.'

She turned and put a hand on his arm, some of the tension leaving her. 'How's your ankle this morning? Would you like me to ice it again?'

'No, it's all right. The swelling's not getting any worse. I think I just need to rest it a while longer.'

She seemed to realise then how close they were standing, how quiet and electric the air had become and how he was looking down at her with the same hungry expression he'd worn the night before, and for one crazy, light-headed moment she considered reaching up and pulling his head down and letting him kiss her.

But then a horn sounded out in the front yard, and she stiffened instead, and her eyebrows shot up from behind her glasses. 'My God!' she said. 'It's them!'

'Already?'

'Well, who else could it be?'

Taking off her apron she folded it over the back of a chair and hurried from the room, patting self-consciously at her honey-blonde hair. Tucking his crutch under his arm, Mitch limped after her.

A vintage flame-red Chevy Camaro had pulled up in the front yard and a man and woman were getting out of it as Agnes forced herself to smile and opened the door.

'Scott!' she called without crossing the threshold. 'What a lovely surprise! I wasn't expecting you until tonight!'

The man, Scott Shelby, came around the car and up the steps to the house. Mitch, wondering how easy he was going to be to fool, studied him closely. He was of average height and chunky build, dressed in smart designer jeans, a rose-coloured safari shirt and expensive grey suede Lanvin sneakers. He had a round, pale face that was a little too heavy around the jowls, with cool blue eyes and a miser's sober mouth. He wore his gelled mid-brown hair in a short, spiky cut.

'I know,' he said as he opened the screen door and stepped inside. 'But there was less traffic than I was expecting, and — '

Noticing Mitch for the first time, his voice dried up.

'Don't apologise,' Agnes told him brightly. 'Your timing's perfect. I get to meet your new wife that much sooner and you get to meet my fiancé, Mitch.'

Turning to Mitch, she said sweetly, 'Honey, this is Scott.'

A fiancé was the last thing Scott had been expecting and the look of surprise on his smooth, near-feminine face was almost comical. Enjoying the moment, Mitch stuck out his hand and said enthusiastically, 'Hi, Scott. Aggie's told me all about you.'

Scott didn't even notice the hand until his wife came inside to join them and gave him a none-too-subtle nudge. 'Sweetie?' she said. 'Where are your manners? Shake the man's hand.'

Scott blinked, then recovered himself and they shook. 'Uh, yes. I'm sorry, I didn't expect . . . Ah, nice to meet you.'

With some difficulty he finally tore his eyes away from Mitch and returned his attention to Agnes. 'Sis,' he said, 'this is Kelly-Anne.'

The two women shook, each evaluating the other.

In her smart pencil skirt and dark keyhole top, Kelly-Anne appeared tall and slender, with slim hips and long legs. She had a long, strong face with direct, intelligent hazel-gold eyes, high, pronounced cheekbones and a straight, confident mouth, and she wore her naturally curly hair swept back from a tiny widow's peak to cascade down across her shoulders and back in a lush, red-auburn spill. Like Scott, she was somewhere in her late twenties.

Sensing Mitch's obvious interest in her, some of Agnes's earlier good humour evaporated and she suddenly became tetchy again. 'Why don't we go into the den?' she suggested stiffly, moving between them and taking Kelly-Anne's arm. 'We've masses to talk about.'

Allowing her eyes to linger a second longer on Mitch, Kelly-Anne said amiably, 'Lead on — sister-in-law.'

6

Agnes served everyone iced tea.

'I didn't put any sweetener in yours,' she told Kelly-Anne. 'I wasn't sure if you used any.'

Kelly-Anne shook her head. 'I don't,' she said, adding with a bold glance in Mitch's direction, 'I try to keep everything I put in my body as natural as possible.'

Recognising a come-on when he saw one, Mitch grinned. 'It shows. A gym rat, right?'

'Five days a week. You?'

'Every chance I get. 'Course, drinking six-packs and sitting behind a wheel all day don't help the waistline.'

Kelly-Anne arched one eyebrow. 'Oh, I don't know. You look perfect to me.'

'He *is* perfect,' Agnes said coolly, serving Scott. 'But I'd love him even if he wasn't.'

Mitch winked at her. 'Back atchya.'

Turning to Scott, he added teasingly, 'Hard to believe, isn't it? That someone as beautiful as your sister could love a dumb trucker like me?'

Scott almost choked on his iced tea. 'Y-you're a *trucker?*'

'Hey, it might not be rocket science, but it suits me. I'm pretty much my own boss, and being out on the open road gives me a real sense of freedom.'

'Not to mention all those lovely muscles,' Kelly-Anne added. She flicked a barbed glance at Scott. 'Maybe you should give up computer programming and take a job outdoors. You might find it . . . beneficial.'

Scott shot her a prissy look. 'I prefer to use my brain. It's what separates us from the animals — in case you've forgotten.'

He frowned suddenly. 'Where's Diana? I hoped she'd be here.'

Agnes sighed. 'Out in the desert. Where else? But I did tell her you were coming.'

'Then she'll be here,' Scott said, adding for Kelly-Anne's benefit, 'We were always close.'

Mitch and Kelly-Anne listened politely

while brother and sister caught up on each other's news. Agnes didn't have much to say for herself, but Scott, who seemed determined to blind them all with science, chatted at great length about source codes and conditional execution, the importance of algorithmic complexity and — of course — failure elimination.

'Isn't that just a fancy term for debugging?' Mitch interrupted suddenly.

Scott broke off in mid-sentence and raised one eyebrow in mild surprise. 'Well . . . yes. I suppose you *could* say that.'

'Then why don't you guys just say 'debugging'?' Mitch deadpanned. 'Why dress it up to sound more important than it really is?'

Scott gave him a quick, uncertain shrug that was almost identical to Agnes's. 'Well, I wouldn't say that it's not important . . . '

'I never said it wasn't important,' said Mitch with a faintly mocking smile. 'I just said that a term like 'failure elimination' makes it sound more important than it actually is.'

He took great pleasure from watching

Scott squirm, and judging from her expression, so did Kelly-Anne. But Agnes was evidently feeling a little more charitable. To get him off the hook, she rose and collected their glasses, which in turn gave Kelly-Anne a chance to say, 'Here, let me help you with those.'

Together they went into the kitchen. There Kelly-Anne rested one hip against the counter and watched as Agnes quickly rinsed the glasses and then stacked them upside-down on the drainer.

'I'm looking forward to meeting Diana,' she said. 'When do you suppose she'll be home?'

'That's anyone's guess,' Agnes replied with a nervous smile. 'I'm afraid Diana runs to her own schedule. She always did. But Scott was right. They always were close, those two. So she'll be here . . . eventually.'

Kelly-Anne peered through the window and made a face at the bleak desert slopes beyond. 'How do you stand it, Agnes?'

'Stand what?'

'This. The isolation. It's so quiet, so . . . *empty.*'

'Oh, don't let Diana hear you say that. The desert is anything but empty. It teems with life, and she'll give you chapter and verse on it if you give her half the chance.'

'Oh, sure,' Kelly-Anne said dismissively. 'Animal life, plant life, insect life. But what about people? How far away are your nearest neighbours?'

Agnes looked blank. 'I've never really thought about it.'

'Perhaps you should. You never know when you might need them.'

'I haven't needed anyone so far. Besides, we have a handyman. And of course, I have Mitch.'

'I guess so. But . . . oh, never mind.'

'No, please. What were you going to say?'

'Well, maybe it's none of my business, but . . . there's a whole wide world out there, just waiting to be discovered. Haven't you ever even been tempted to go out and experience it all for yourself? To shop? Go see a movie? Dine out every so often? Take in a show?'

'Of course I have.' Agnes went to the

fridge and took out her bag of fresh white gloves. 'But where's the point, really? At the end of the day, this is home. No other place will ever feel that way to me now. It's been too long.'

'And Diana?'

'Diana has the desert,' Agnes replied simply. 'Ever since Momma died, that's all she's ever wanted, and all she seems to need.'

'Is that what she says?'

Agnes peeled off her old gloves, threw them in the laundry hamper then washed her hands thoroughly. 'If you don't mind my saying so,' she said slowly, weighing every word as she slipped on another pair of gloves, 'you ask an awful lot of questions, Kelly-Anne.'

'I'm sorry. I don't mean to. I suppose I just want to get to know you, get to know what makes you tick, feel like part of the family.'

She reached up and ran her fingers through her hair. 'God, it's hot,' she said.

'Why don't you go up and take a shower?'

'That,' said Scott, appearing in the

doorway, 'sounds like a great idea. You've put us in my old room, I take it?'

'Yes.'

'Come on, then, Kell'. I'll get our bags, we can freshen up and then I'll show you around.'

Kelly-Anne glanced out the window again; and as she left the kitchen to help Scott with their luggage, Agnes heard her murmur softly, 'Yippee.'

⋆   ⋆   ⋆

Kelly-Anne took one look at Scott's room and said sourly, 'I can see this is going to be a fun honeymoon.'

The bright, almost harsh sunshine streaming in through the window did its best to cheer the place up. But like the rest of the house, the room was a hangover from better times past: dull, old-fashioned and ever-so-slightly frayed around the edges.

Scott threw their cases on one of the two single beds and jerked away uncomfortably when Kelly-Anne made a playful grab for his butt.

'Cut that out!' he snapped.

She feigned surprise and then reached for him again. 'What, aren't I even allowed to goose my little honey-bun now?'

Scott avoided her. 'No!'

She shook her head and mocked him. 'Oh, momma, you were right — he *is* gay.'

'For chrissake, Kelly, keep your fucking voice down! They'll *hear* you!'

'Oh, puh-lease. No-one's going to think you're gay, not when you're married to *these*.'

She whipped up her top, revealing superb, natural breasts, each one tipped with a sharp, dark nipple.

Unmoved by the sight, Scott continued with the unpacking.

Needled by his lack of reaction, she covered up again and said coldly: 'That is unless you can't control your hormones and hit on that gorgeous hunk downstairs.'

He glared at her. 'You know, for a psychiatrist, you really *need* a psychiatrist.'

'Didn't you know? We've always been

our own best customers.'

'I believe it. Besides,' he added, 'even if I did fancy him, what chance would I have, the way you were coming on to him?'

'In case you missed it, sweetie, it wasn't all one-sided.'

'The poor guy's probably desperate for it,' he countered. 'I don't suppose Agnes has allowed him anything more than a peck on the cheek so far.'

'Ooh, careful, kitty-cat, your claws are showing.'

'Never mind my claws,' he warned her as she kicked off her Guiseppe Zanotti sandals, took out her toiletry bag and went into the bathroom. 'Just stay away from that cretin. You piss Agnes off and she'll throw us both out of here. Then the weekend really *will* be a total bust.'

'It may be a bust, anyway.'

He frowned, stopped unpacking and followed her as far as the bathroom door. 'What's that supposed to mean?'

'It means that your beloved sister may be a recluse. She may even be slightly neurotic. But from what I've seen of her so far, she doesn't appear to be at all schizophrenic.'

'What about washing her hands day and night, and wearing those white gloves?'

Kelly-Anne shrugged. 'Allergies?'

'Not according to Diana. She says Agnes's hands are fine.'

'Okay, so she's a mysophobe. So was Howard Hughes, and no judge ever ruled *him* incapable of handling his own affairs.'

'So make something up,' he told her.

'Oh, no,' she retorted. 'I told you when you first came to me with this idea that my larcenous streak only goes so far. I'll evaluate her, and I'll try to find legitimate psychological reasons to declare her incompetent, but I won't lie. It's too risky. If I get caught, I lose my licence.'

A rare, chilly smile touched his normally sober lips. 'When we find the gold that's buried around here, you won't *need* a licence. You'll be too busy shopping in Scottsdale and taking 'round-the-world cruises.'

'Maybe I will,' she said. 'But until we

do find it, all I have right now is fifty percent of *nothing*. And like I told you at the outset, Scottie *dear*, I didn't spend seven years studying psychiatry just to end up working at the local Dairy Queen.'

★   ★   ★

Mel Crane parked his car in front of the diner, climbed out and carefully donned his pearl-grey Stetson.

In the enervating pre-noon heat, Shelby's Oasis was still and silent but for the ticking of the Tahoe's cooling engine. There was no sign of Agnes Shelby's hired man, Neon, and no sign of his car — an old yellow VW Beetle, Crane seemed to recall.

Hitching up his pants, the sheriff gave his isolated surroundings one final, quick inspection. He then began to root more diligently around each of the three run-down buildings, looking for anything that might give him a lead on Agnes Shelby's mysterious burglar. But it was hard to find the enthusiasm for the job.

For as long as he could remember,

Crane had wanted to be a cop. He'd joined the Tucson Police Department straight out of college and slowly worked his way up from patrol officer to criminal investigator, from narcotics agent to administration captain, from uniform patrol captain to Watch Commander, and he'd loved every damn' second of it.

The only place left to go after that had been County Sheriff, an elected post that being a well-known local boy and staunch Republican to boot, he'd won by a landslide.

It should have been the highlight of his career. But instead it was and always would be over-shadowed by the death of his beloved wife, Mabel.

Funny really, he thought as he did his best to concentrate on the investigation at hand. Three years on, and he was as helpless now to deal with the pain of losing her as he'd been the day she finally closed her tired grey eyes and just slipped away from him.

They'd met at high school and married a year after graduation. She had been a smart, articulate, fun-loving girl given to deep thought and careful decision, and Crane had known from the outset that in Mabel Teresa Bell he'd found everything he could ever want in a partner.

Sure enough, she'd supported him all through his steady climb to the top and never once asked anything in return. She'd never uttered a word of complaint about the stresses, strains and uncertainties a cop's wife had to face day after day, never grumbled when he worked late into the night (which was often), or when he had to choose between work and family life and invariably chose work.

It galled him now to think that he'd given her so little in return. Instead he'd become so wrapped up in his own career, trying to be the best he could possibly be, that after a time he'd just taken her for granted.

It was only afterward that he realised how old she'd grown, and how thin . . .

It turned out that she'd discovered a lump in her right breast but typically for her hadn't said a word to him about it; just went and got it checked out — discreetly, of course — all by herself. It had proved to be malignant and her oncologist had wanted to admit her to hospital and operate immediately.

Incredibly, Mabel had said no, not right then. Her beloved Mel was midway through his campaign and she was afraid that her troubles might distract him and maybe cost him the election — as if the election was somehow more important to him than she was.

So she'd kept it all to herself. She'd continued to show up at every function and smile politely and support him just as staunchly as she'd always done; and only when it was all over and he was sworn in as the new County Sheriff did she sit him down and tell him that she was sick, that she needed an operation but not to worry, because everything was going to be okay.

It wasn't, though.

By the time they got ready to remove the lump, the cancer had spread — metastasized, they called it. They found it in her lymph nodes, in her bones, in her liver and lungs and brain.

God.

The only good thing you could say for

it was that it killed her quick; and unless you counted the almost unimaginable hell of knowing that you could measure your life in weeks if not days, then she didn't suffer the way some folks did.

Crane suffered, though.

Riddled with guilt, believing that he should have guessed something was wrong and probably *would* have if only he'd taken more notice of what was going on around him, he'd suffered every minute of every hour of every day since it happened; and if it weren't for the sacrifice Mabel had made to get him where he was, he'd have happily eaten a bullet in order to join her.

But Mabel never would have condoned that. She'd have wanted him to carry on and be the best sheriff he could be, no matter how hard he might find it now that she was no longer at his side. And for that reason he'd squared his wide shoulders and set about doing just that.

A stronger or more determined man might have made a go of it. But without Mabel, Crane's strength and determination seemed to desert him. Only now that she was gone did he fully realise what she had always meant to him, and just how lost he was without her.

And there, he thought, was the true heart of the matter.

The job, the calling to which he'd devoted the whole of his adult life, had ended up costing him everything, and for that reason he'd grown to despise it. And so, without even really being aware of it, he'd begun to do exactly what they said he did — he'd just started going through the motions.

For three years he'd done that.

Now he had only one year left to serve of his four-year tenure, unless of course they retired him ahead of time because he was finding it increasingly impossible to disguise his lack of commitment. He'd already heard such whispers.

But who gave a damn about that? Perhaps if he'd thought a little more about Mabel and what *she* had wanted from life instead of just focusing on his *own* goals . . .

But hell, it was too late now.

Too late . . .

He stopped searching, straightened up, stretched his back and then pinched at the skin between his close-set eyes. God, he was tired. In fact, he was more than tired: he was somehow *broken*, and it was a god-awful feeling.

At the back of the diner he found a truck hidden under a tarp just where Agnes Shelby had said it was. He lifted the edge of the tarp, identified the vehicle as old Flapjack Shelby's red Ford pickup and then whipped the cover back off the hood. Shading his eyes with his hat, he peered in through the dusty windshield and saw that the keys were still hanging from the ignition.

He was shaking his head in disapproval when his attention was claimed by an almost inaudible chirruping sound that, as near as he could tell, seemed to come from inside the snake-farm.

Remembering how concerned Agnes had been about her missing cat, he dropped the tarp back over the pickup, put his hat back on and retraced his steps until he came to the front of the snake-farm itself.

Long before he got there he spotted a stick lying in the dirt just outside the doorway. He bent and examined it without touching it. It looked like a mop- or broom-handle that had snapped in half.

He made a more careful inspection of his surroundings. Propped against the corner of the building he found a short length of planking with a dark, dry stain at one end. He smelled the stain, then slipped on a disposable glove and touched his finger to it. The tip came away red.

Blood?

Chirrup.

He glanced around, his thoughts returning to the missing cat. Shoving back to his feet and peeling the glove off, he pulled the snake-farm door open and stepped inside.

Despite the jagged holes in the roof, through which sunshine fell in dusty bars, the air was stuffy and warm, and stank unmistakably of putrescence. He glanced at the glass cases and their long-dead occupants and took out a kerchief, which he held over his nose and mouth.

'Benji?' he called.

A low, plaintive chirrup came from the far end of the building.

He frowned thoughtfully. Unless he was mistaken, it sounded as if the creature was stuck behind one of the cases at the end of the building and couldn't get himself free.

'Benji?'

This time there was no response.

Crane walked slowly, carefully, in and out of light and shadow until he reached the end of the building. When he reached the very last cage he took off his beloved Stetson and peered into the darkness behind it.

He exhaled softly.

There was nothing there save cobwebs and dust.

And yet . . .

And yet he couldn't shake the feeling that he was being watched by . . . *something*.

The cat?

That was the hell of it: he didn't think so.

The feeling suddenly became so strong

that he turned quickly, brushed the left-side fold of his jacket aside and closed his big right fist around the grips of his Glock 22.40.

As near as he could tell, he was all alone. But there was *something* about this ramshackle home of the dead that gave him the creeps, made him feel that there was danger here, a danger he couldn't seem to identify.

The place made him feel slightly claustrophobic and he wanted to quit it in a hurry, but he was damned if he'd do so. He'd leave the way he entered, nice and slow.

In that moment he heard — or *thought* he heard — something behind him, and again he spun on his heel, this time expecting to see the long-lost cat at last.

He was just in time to see something moving fast along the outside shack wall, its form momentarily blocking out the strips of sunshine that showed between the loose-fitting planks.

Keeping his eyes on the shadows at the far end of the shack, he backed slowly, purposefully, toward the sagging door. He was almost there when he heard a heavy thump behind him, followed by a sharp, sudden rattle.

Recognising the second sound, he whirled around, his eyes dropping to the worn floorboards just inside the doorway.

A black-tailed rattlesnake was slowly uncoiling on the dusty floorboards.

He drew a sharp breath and backed up a pace.

As beautiful as it was deadly, the snake must have measured at least four feet from the tip of its flat head to the last, segmented rattle on its pure black tail. Its fat, golden-yellow body, patterned along the back by a series of gradually-fading black diamonds, appeared to shine in the harsh sunlight as its front end slowly began to ooze across the floor toward him.

The rattler looked mad enough to strike, and as he took another backward step he wondered why that should be. The black-tail wasn't any more aggressive than any other snake. You left *him* alone, he generally left *you* alone.

But then he thought about that

thumping sound.

Had someone thrown the snake into the building, knowing he was in there? Was it someone's idea of a sick practical joke?

Whose?

The person he thought he'd spotted moving along the outer wall?

The snake began to lift up, regarding him with its bright, beady eyes. Its thin, forked black tongue flickered as its jaws parted slightly. Crane didn't know for sure exactly what it was planning, but knew better than to wait and find out.

Mouth firming down, he drew his piece, took aim and fired twice. His first bullet missed and ripped splinters from the floorboards behind the rattler. The second .40-calibre rimless cartridge hit the mark, and the rattler's head exploded in a chunky red mist. The body flipped, then wriggled and twisted over and in on itself, revealing a lighter underside, the rattle still whirring angrily.

Leathering the Glock, Crane stepped over the snake and hustled back out into the sunshine. He was sweating.

He took off his hat and mopped his face with the kerchief. Before he put it away, he gave the sweatband of his hat a wipe, too.

Then he froze.

The stick or broom-handle or whatever it had been was gone.

So was the blood-stained plank.

He whistled softly.

Then he hurried back to the Tahoe, climbed inside, gunned the engine and sent the vehicle bouncing down the trail toward the Shelby place.

Three people had gathered on the porch, drawn outside by the sound of the shots. He wheeled the vehicle to a halt beside a flame-red Camaro and then climbed out.

'It's okay, folks,' he said, grabbing up his hat and keeping his tone casual. 'Nothing to worry about! Just had to explain the facts of life to a rattler.'

Mitch showed him a grin that was just this side of insolent. 'You wasted a bullet, sheriff. All the snakes up there are dead.'

'They are now,' Crane said. Tipping his hat to the stunning redhead standing beside Scott Shelby, he added, 'Howdy, Scott. Been a spell.'

Scott nodded. 'Business has kept me humping.'

Allowing his dark eyes to linger on Kelly-Anne, Crane said, 'I'm sure it has.'

Realising that no one was going to introduce her, Kelly-Anne said to Crane: 'I'm Kelly-Anne. Scott's wife.'

Surprise arched his eyebrows. 'Sheriff Crane, ma'am. Pleasure.'

'What brings you out here today, sheriff?' asked Mitch.

'Just my job, son. Oh, and, uh, you might want to take the keys out of old Flapjack's ignition. Wouldn't want that, ah, burglar, driving off with it.'

Scott looked at Mitch. 'Burglar?'

Mitch shrugged as if it were no big deal. 'Yeah. A guy broke in here last night. Agnes and Diana got the drop on him and managed to tie him up, but he got loose and took off before the sheriff could get here.'

Kelly-Anne looked uneasily at the surrounding slopes. 'Well, I hope he doesn't come back.'

'I doubt that he will, ma'am,' Crane assured her. 'What do you reckon, son? You think he'll be back?'

Mitch boldly met his gaze. 'Why ask me? I'm a trucker, not a cop.'

'Is Miss Agnes around?'

'Inside.'

'I'd like to see her, if I may.'

'Sure. Come on in.'

As they went in out of the sun, Agnes appeared from the kitchen. Seeing Crane, she faltered briefly, then said: 'Sheriff! Do you, uh, have any news?'

'In a way,' he replied vaguely.

'Oh?'

He nodded to the others. 'I hope the rest of you folks'll excuse me, but . . . I'd like to speak with Miss Agnes in private, if I may.'

Agnes turned to Mitch. He frowned briefly at the back of the sheriff's head and then gave her a faint nod.

In the den, with the door closed behind them, she poured Crane a glass of cool lemonade and he took a sip. 'Ahh, perfect. I swear, Miss Agnes, you make a fine glass of lemonade. Just enough lemon to make it tart without, you know, puckering the lips.'

Agnes brushed the compliment aside. 'Thank you. But ... I don't want to appear rude, but ... what exactly was it you wanted to see me about, sheriff?'

'Mitch Akins,' he said softly.

'My fiancé? What about him?'

'Did you know he's got a rap sheet?'

'A what?'

'A criminal record.'

'Mitch has been in trouble with the police?' She fell silent for a moment before shaking her head. 'I find that very hard to believe.'

'Well, it's true, ma'am. I ran a check on him myself, and computers don't lie.'

She made an agitated gesture with her gloved hands. 'Well, what's he supposed to have done?'

Crane took another sip of lemonade. 'Joy-riding, petty theft, a burglary charge that was dropped for lack of evidence. Stuff like that.'

'Nothing serious, then,' she said, relieved.

'Meaning he hasn't killed anyone yet?'

Crane smiled. 'No. Leastways, no-one we know of. But that doesn't mean he isn't capable of it.'

Agnes stiffened righteously. '*Everyone* is capable of it, sheriff. Even you and I.'

'True. But it comes a little easier for some than it does for others.'

'I daresay. But Mitch isn't the violent type. And since we're about to be married, *I* should know.' She moved to the door. 'Of course, I thank you for stopping by to tell me all this, sheriff. As usual, I see that you're right on top of things.'

Crane didn't move. 'What are you going to do about it? Now that you know?'

'What would you *have* me do? Jilt him?' She shook her head. 'I love Mitch and he loves me. If he has a past, well, so be it. We all have our skeletons to hide.' She opened the door, adding coolly, 'Now, if that's *all*, sheriff . . . '

'Actually,' he said, 'it's not.'

'Oh?'

'No. I was wondering where Neon is right now?'

She shrugged. 'I told you before. Sometimes he goes into town and stays over for a night or two.'

'When do you expect him back?'

'Tonight, maybe. Early tomorrow.'

'I see. Thank you, ma'am.' Draining his glass, he complimented her one final time on her lemonade, then gently set his Stetson atop his head and left without a backward glance.

7

Reluctant to spend any more time with Scott than he had to — although it would have been a different prospect where Kelly-Anne was concerned — Mitch excused himself and hobbled up to his room.

He stretched out on the bed and crossed his arms behind his head. Crane worried him. He gave the impression that he knew more than he was letting on. It was probably standard cop procedure, and he was probably like it with everyone, but if for whatever reason Crane wanted to rattle him, he was doing a good job of it.

In any case, Mitch wanted a few quiet moments to think about the newspaper clipping he'd found pasted to the back of Old Man Shelby's picture. He'd snuck into the den earlier that morning to take a better look at it, and it had made very interesting reading.

Clipped from an old copy of the

Phoenix *Sun*, it was headlined LOCAL PROSPECTOR FOUND DEAD IN SUPERSTITION MOUNTAINS. The article went on to say:

The body of Henry 'Flapjack' Shelby, whom many believe to have found the legendary Lost Dutchman Mine, was discovered yesterday by hikers. A coroner's autopsy revealed that he had been dead for several days. Death was the result of a fall from a ledge onto some rocks. Foul play is not suspected.

Shelby is survived by his son, Scott, and twin daughters, Agnes and Diana.

Mitch wondered exactly where 'Flapjack' had been when he fell to his death. Anywhere near the mine he'd supposedly discovered? It was always possible. He wondered if Agnes knew, and whether or not she'd be prepared to tell him. He'd have to ask. It might be a good place to start searching.

Before he could consider the matter further, he heard footsteps hurrying along the landing outside. A moment later, Agnes burst in without knocking and closed the door swiftly behind her.

Her face was dark as a thunderstorm.

Keeping his tone casual, he said, 'Sheriff gone?'

She stood there for a moment before saying angrily: 'Why didn't you tell me you'd been in trouble with the police?'

Mitch sat up, disgusted. 'So *that's* why Sherlock was here, huh? To rat me out.' He swung his legs over the edge of the bed and sat up. 'Did he also tell you that all that happened when I was just a kid?'

'No. But that's not the point. You should've told me. Then I could have just shrugged it off. Now . . . well, now he knows we keep secrets from each other.'

'So what? It's your brother we're trying to con, not some guy whose biggest problem is keeping his fucking *hat* clean.'

'Please, Mitch, I asked you not to swear.'

'All right, all right.'

He moved restlessly to the window in

order to hide the tell-tale mark Diana's knife had cut into the frame. He felt Agnes watching him closely and hated the sensation. Presently she asked quietly, 'Is there . . . anything *else* important that I should know about you?'

He shrugged, some of his old belligerence boiling back to the surface. 'Only that I'm pretty good in the sack.'

Her body went rigid, and she turned and reached for the door handle.

Losing patience with her, he snapped, 'What is it, are you allergic to fucking, too?'

She flung open the door and rushed out. He called after her but she didn't reply, and moments later he heard the slam of her bedroom door.

Shit!

He hated the way she had of making him feel bad, hated feeling bad because it wasn't something he'd ever really felt much before. Reluctantly he got to his feet, grabbed his crutch and limped across the landing to her room.

He opened the door. Her bedroom was a revelation to him, all pastel pinks and delicate white furniture and frilly curtains and stuffed cats. A little girl's room.

Agnes herself was on her bed, crying into her pillows. He entered, closed the door and said softly: 'I'm sorry. I didn't mean what I said.'

He watched her shoulders work. She was crying silently, and in a way that was worse than if she'd been wailing.

'I'm not mad at *you*,' he said. 'It's that damn' sheriff I'm pissed at. The sonofabitch's out to get me and I don't know why.'

Agnes sat up, sniffed, dabbed at her eyes with her gloved hands and then picked up her glasses from the bedside table. 'It doesn't matter,' she said as she slipped them back on. 'I d-don't care about your p-past, and I told him so. It's how you treat me *now* that matters.'

He came close, reached down, took her gently by the arms and helped her stand. She came up slowly, nervously, knowing instinctively what was going to happen next.

He pulled her close, kissed her. At first she tried to resist, as he'd known she would. But he knew also that any resistance would only be for show, and that it wouldn't last.

It didn't.

In the next moment he felt her respond, thrust herself against him, melt into his embrace and kiss him back with increasing urgency. Her mouth opened, he tasted her tongue, felt himself stirring and was vaguely surprised that this ghost-pale, anxiety-ridden woman could do that to him.

At last they broke apart. He looked into her face, saw his own flushed features distorted in the lenses of her glasses and went to kiss her again —

This time, however, she pushed him away. She'd returned to her default setting: fluster mode. 'No, don't . . . ' she whispered.

'What's the matter? Frightened you might get to like it?'

Her expression hardened. 'Get out,' she hissed.

He shrugged, annoyed as much with himself as with her, then stormed out, door slamming behind him.

Once he was gone, Agnes heard a sound behind her and turned with a start. Diana was standing in the bathroom doorway, looking tall and lithe in her cut-offs and short, loose top, her body tanned to the colour of a new penny, her skin free of any blemish, her expression at once disdainful, predatory, jealous.

'Y-you can't have him,' Agnes said nervously. 'He's mine.'

Diana didn't reply. She didn't need to. Her expression, her eyes, her stance . . . these things said it all for her.

Keep away.

But Agnes was damned if she would! Mitch was *her* man, her fiancé, and she was going to keep him! She said venomously: 'I mean it, Diana. Leave him alone. Leave me alone.'

Diana continued to stand picture-still and silent in the bathroom doorway.

'You'll never win,' Agnes said, teeth gritted. 'You can't. Want to know why?'

Diana raised one perfect eyebrow expectantly.

'Because I'll *kill* him before I let you have him,' Agnes said in a way that suggested she relished the prospect. 'I *swear* I will.'

★ ★ ★

When Benji still hadn't shown up by dusk, Agnes asked Mitch to go out and find him.

Ever since she'd told him to get out of her room, their relationship had been cool and distant; and to his surprise Mitch realised that he hated it probably as much as he felt sure Agnes did.

To make peace with her, he solemnly promised that he'd search high and low until he found her missing cat, and that earned him a grateful forgiving smile. 'By the way,' he added as he went out the door, 'how come Benji makes that strange chirruping sound?'

'He's a Chartreux,' Agnes explained. 'They all do it. They hardly ever meow. Instead they make a sweet little chirrup that sometimes ends in a purr.'

Leaving the porch and leaning heavily on his crutch, Mitch made his way up the brushy rise that overlooked the house from the west, calling Benji's name every few yards.

'Goddammit, where *are* you, you idiot cat?' he grumbled after ten frustrating minutes. He stopped as he saw a barely-discernible path that led between large rocks, and struggled to climb higher in order to reach it.

The trail led around to a cleared shelf of sandy ground about thirty feet square, dotted here and there with a dozen foot-high, weathered wooden crosses. Mitch stopped and frowned down at them, then went a little closer and, by the amber light of the setting sun, began to read the crude inscriptions carved into each one.

Cookie . . . Milly . . . Sophie . . . Rocky . . . Trespass . . .

After a moment he realised that this was a pet cemetery: that each of these crosses marked the final resting-place of a former Shelby pet. And if the names were anything to go by, they'd all been cats.

He glanced around, hoping to find Benji nearby. It would certainly put him back in Agnes's good graces if he could bring the cat home safe and sound like he'd promised. But even as the thought occurred to him, he wondered why that should be so important to him.

And yet it *was*.

But there was no sign of the cat. He moved on, climbing ever higher, failing to see the hunched, slate-grey Chartreux watching him from the shadows clustered around the farthest grave.

The cat hissed softly at his departing back.

★ ★ ★

'Any sign of him?' Agnes asked anxiously as Mitch re-entered the house an hour later.

'Uh-uh. And before you ask, I searched everywhere. Maybe you should go out there? If he hears your voice . . . ?'

She made no reply, but continued to watch the darkening landscape worriedly through the screen door, her gloved hands knitting together.

'Do you think the coyotes might've got him?' he asked.

'I don't know *what* to think. But I wish Diana would come back. She'd know where to find him.'

He realised then that she was close to tears. 'Isn't there any way you can reach her?'

She gave her head a nervous shake. 'No. She won't use a cell phone, even if we could get a signal way out here. She says it would disturb the serenity of the desert.'

He started to say something but she cut him off with, 'Please, don't look like that. I know Diana can be . . . well, strange, at times. But for all her faults I love her dearly, and I want you to love her as well. After all, you're part of the family now. We have to stick together.'

That said, she turned and padded back toward the kitchen, where she'd been fixing the evening meal.

* * *

That night one of the region's periodic electrical storms swept across the desert. With it came strong winds that battered

123

the Oasis, rattled loose doors and shutters and howled on around the Shelby house itself.

Sometime after midnight, Diana glided along the shadowy landing to Mitch's door, holding a beautiful desert poppy in her hands. As she reached for the handle, a low, ominous chirrup halted her in her tracks.

Down at the far end of the hall, she saw two small copper eyes watching her from the darkness.

She and the cat traded murderous stares for a long moment. The only sounds were the howling of the wind, the soft, grating sounds of sand scratching at the windows, the occasional dry crackle of forked lightning stamping itself into the earth.

Finally she reached for the handle again, and again the cat released a low, menacing chirrup.

Diana faced the creature. Her shoulders came up, the fingers of her free hand twisted into claws, her chin tucked down and she glared at the cat from under lowered brows.

Benji never moved; never blinked.

Unfazed, Diana turned her back on him. Kneeling, she left the poppy outside Mitch's door and then cat-footed back the way she'd come.

★　★　★

Mid-morning of the following day, Kelly-Anne found Mitch seated in a chair on the front porch. He was bracing his crutch against the nearest post in order to keep the chair tipped back on its two rear legs.

'Trying to break your other ankle?' she asked by way of greeting.

He grinned as she joined him. He wore the poppy tucked into the pocket of his denim jacket, figuring that Agnes had left it for him, and that she'd be pleased to see him wearing it.

'I'm pretending to be Wyatt Earp,' he said.

'Excuse me?'

'Ever watch old westerns on TV?'

'Uh-uh.'

'There's this great John Ford movie,

My Darling Clementine. It's all about the gunfight at the OK Corral. In one scene, Henry Fonda, who's Wyatt Earp, is sitting outside his office, chair tilted back, keeping himself balanced by pushing off with his feet on the post in front of him.'

'The point being . . . ?'

'No point. Just Fonda stealing a scene.'

'Oh.'

Kelly-Anne turned and leaned against the rail so that her butt poked cutely in his direction. 'God,' she said, 'this place gives me the willies. You two aren't going to stay here after you're married, are you?'

'We haven't really discussed it. But I can't see myself raising snakes for a hobby.'

She turned to him. She was dressed as stylishly — and expensively — as she had been the previous day, in a loose, gold-striped white shirt and yellow Valencia shorts. 'Would you like to show me around?' she asked suddenly. 'Or are you too busy being Wyatt Earp?'

Looking at her and seeing all kinds of positives in being her tour guide, Mitch set his chair down gently and got slowly to his feet. 'Sure I'll show you around,' he smiled. 'Let's go.'

★　★　★

They didn't get any further than the gas station before they started kissing.

The electricity between them had been impossible to ignore. She wanted him as much as he wanted her and they both knew it, so there was no need for a slow build-up. Almost as soon as they were out of sight of the house they were in each other's arms, kissing hungrily, her hands working their way urgently toward the crotch of his pants, his hands grabbing her by the hair, cradling her butt, mashing her groin against his.

The desert poppy fell from his pocket and was trampled underfoot as he shoved her against the gas station wall and started fumbling with the buttons of her shirt. He was so intent on getting to her that it was several seconds before he realised that she had stiffened in his arms, was no longer allowing their mutual

127

need to carry her along: that she was actually pushing him away from her.

'What's wrong?' he said, stepping back.

He realised then that she wasn't even looking at him, she was looking at something — *someone* — behind them.

He turned fast, afraid that it might be Agnes, but instead he saw a short, dumpy black man aiming a twelve-gauge shotgun at them from nearby.

Skin blanching, Mitch turned to face him full-on and brought his hands up, saying, 'Easy, there, friend! That sucker could go off . . . '

The black man looked as nervous as Mitch felt. He said in a low, gravelly voice, 'You gonna give me a *reason* to make it go off?'

'No way, man.'

'What you all doin' here?'

Kelly-Anne peered at him over Mitch's shoulder. 'J-Just looking around.'

'Lookin' around?' the black man repeated sceptically. 'Or *trespassin'*? Looks to me more like the latter.'

'We're not trespassing,' Kelly-Anne said quickly. 'We're guests here. At least *I* am.' Indicating Mitch, she added, 'He's engaged to the woman who owns this place.'

The black man frowned. He was about sixty, with large, pouchy eyes and a wide mouth full of big gold teeth. His hair was dusted white at the temples, the whites of his eyes more accurately a dull yellow. 'Then why he out here with you?'

It was a good question.

'I was, uh, showing her around,' Mitch said lamely. 'Isn't that right?'

'Yes,' Kelly-Anne said. 'And I . . . I suddenly felt faint and . . . and he caught me just before I collapsed.'

She could see by his expression that she was still a long way from convincing him, so she brought up her left hand and flashed her wedding ring at him. 'I'm Mrs Shelby, Scott's wife. Mitch, tell him who Scott is — '

'I know who Mr Scott is,' said the black man. 'I'm Neon.'

'*Neon?*'

'Miss Agnes's handyman.'

'Well, now that we all know each other,' said Mitch, reaching for his crutch, 'you can put that shotgun down, Neon.'

The black man made no attempt to do so.

'Look, it's easy enough to check out,' said Mitch. 'Let's all go down to the house and ask Agnes.'

Neon considered that for a moment before finally nodding and easing down the hammers on the twelve-gauge. 'All right,' he said. 'Come on. And no tricks.'

'You've been watching too much TV,' said Mitch. He limped away from Kelly-Anne, adding: 'You go on ahead and tell Agnes we'll be right along.'

She frowned at him, but when he nodded she edged past Neon and started off in the direction of the house. Despite the circumstances Mitch couldn't help but admire the view she presented.

He fell into step beside Neon. Together they followed Kelly-Anne back past the snake-farm and down toward the house.

'How long you worked here, Neon?'

'Since before they built the new highway.'

'Then you knew Flapjack Shelby?'

'Sure. He hired me, on account of I like snakes.'

'Did you run the snake-farm?'

'Till folks stopped comin', yeah.'

'And then?'

Neon shrugged. 'When the business went belly-up, Mr Shelby, he couldn't pay me no more. If it hadn't been for Miss Agnes, I don't know *what* I'd'a done. Said if I'd help out around here, she'd feed me and let me live in the diner. So I — '

'You live in the *diner?*' Mitch said incredulously.

'Sure. Fixed up the storeroom real fine,' he said proudly.

'And this was before or after Flapjack found the gold?'

Neon gave him a wary look from under knitted brows.

'You can tell me, Neon,' Mitch coaxed. 'Hell, I'm almost part of the family.'

'Why don't you ask Miss Agnes yourself, then?'

''Cause I'm asking you,' Mitch said, his voice hardening. 'Now, give, old man.'

Neon opened his mouth and was just about to respond when Kelly-Anne, who had vanished into the house, now came back out onto the porch and waved at them.

'Mitch! Neon! Agnes says lunch is ready!'

Neon sagged, relieved. Mitch grinned and waved back at her. When he turned back to Neon, however, the grin faded and he said, 'Better not keep 'em waiting, I guess. But we'll talk some more about this later. You got that . . . *friend?*'

He limped toward the house with Neon hurrying after him.

★　★　★

She might have been a fruitcake, but Agnes was also one hell of a good cook. Even Kelly-Anne had to admit that when lunch came to an end.

'That was wonderful, Agnes. I'm stuffed.'

'Me too,' added Mitch. 'Really hit the spot, hon.'

Enjoying the praise, Agnes fairly preened. 'How about you, Scottie? More chicken salad?'

'No, thanks.'

Scott had other things on his mind. Glancing at Neon, he said, 'When you were driving back from town, I don't suppose you saw any sign of Diana?'

Picking food from between his gold teeth, Neon shook his head. 'No, sir. And I took the Old Back Road, too. They's a new litter of coyote pups in one of the caves around there where she sometimes hangs out.'

Scott scowled impatiently. 'I was certain she'd be here by now.' He gave Agnes a stern look. 'You're *sure* you told her we were coming?'

'Of course,' she said.

'I was there when she did it,' said Mitch. When Agnes looked at him, he winked.

Kelly-Anne said, 'Well, I hope she shows up soon. I'm dying to meet her. From what Scott's told me, she sounds fascinating.'

'She is,' confirmed Agnes. 'And so kind and . . . thoughtful. After Papa died, I never could have stayed on here without her help.'

Scott leaned back from the table, his

mind elsewhere. 'Strange. Last time *I* spoke to her, I got the impression she wanted to leave — and would've, too, if you hadn't kicked up such a fuss about it.'

The sweet smile Agnes had bestowed upon Mitch shrivelled as she turned back to her brother. 'Dear Scottie,' she said sweetly, 'as usual you've got everything twisted around.'

'Have I?'

Glancing at Kelly-Anne, Agnes said, 'Remember yesterday, when I told you that this is home for me?'

'Yes.'

'I really meant it. It *is* home. But more than that, it's home for Diana. She loves this wild country, and I suppose I love it because she loves it. But if it weren't for her, I'd leave this place like a shot, for the good of my health.'

'Your health?'

Agnes raised her gloved hands. 'I have a skin condition. A condition that could improve if I were to move to a cooler, moister climate.'

'Oh.'

'Would *you* fight to stay in a place where you itch day and night and your skin looks more like that of an alligator? No,' she continued, answering her own question. 'And neither would I. If Diana really wanted to leave, I'd pack up and be gone by tomorrow. But contrary to what Scottie here would have you believe, she doesn't want to go. And because she wants to stay, *I* stay.'

In the heavy silence that followed, Mitch reached out and took one of her hands between both his. 'Well,' he said, 'they may not be the prettiest hands in the world, but I don't care. It's what's inside that makes you so special.'

Kelly-Anne said, 'Aw, that's so sweet.' And to Scott, somewhat harder, 'I wish *you'd* be romantic like that.'

Scott's only response was a scowl.

8

The romantic theme continued later that afternoon, when Mitch passed Agnes's room, glanced in and spotted her brushing her honey-blonde hair at the vanity table mirror.

He hobbled inside, grinned at her reflection, and when she spotted him she stopped brushing. He came up behind her, reached down, took her shoulders in his palms and, after the briefest hesitation, began to knead them gently, his touch little more than the lightest brushing of flesh against flesh.

It made Agnes purr like a kitten. 'Mmmm. That does feel good. You've got wonderfully strong hands, you know.'

'Comes from handling an eighteen-wheeler.'

'What an exciting life,' Agnes said dreamily. 'Driving across the country, seeing all those different towns, eating in diners, waitresses hot for your body.' She giggled like a naughty schoolgirl enjoying lewd thoughts. 'You're like a modern-day Ulysses.'

He looked questioningly at her reflection. 'Who?'

'Ulysses. He was a Greek god. Homer wrote about his voyages in his poem, *The Odyssey*. Ulysses had his sirens: you have your waitresses.'

Mitch smiled sourly. 'Oh, sure. 'Cept I'm no god, Greek or otherwise. And the only voyages I ever took were through Greasy Spoon Country by way of Indigestion Highway.'

Agnes shook her head reprovingly. 'Men! Why must you always deal in reality?'

He kissed the top of her head. 'So that beautiful girls like you can get off on love and romance.'

She half-turned, reached up, set one of her hands over one of his.

'What is it?' he asked.

She gave another shake of the head. 'Nothing. I just like looking at you.'

She fell quiet again; then a few moments later said: 'Wouldn't it be romantic, though? You break into my house, intending to rob me, and instead we end up falling in love?'

'It'd be cool, all right. There's just one problem.'

'Which is . . . ?'

'I couldn't live here.'

Agnes shrugged. 'Maybe we wouldn't *have* to.'

'Mean you really would move? What would Diana have to say about that?'

'Oh, she'd be happy for me. She's always teasing me about dying an old maid. Besides, she wouldn't be alone. Neon would be here to look after her.'

'You wouldn't actually *sell* this place, then?'

'Never. But if you're worried about money, don't be.' Lowering her voice, she added confidentially, 'I have plenty.'

Plenty.

The word burned itself into his mind like a hot brand on a spring calf.

'Don't stop,' she said, sinking her head back into her shoulders and closing her eyes. 'Your hands feel so good . . . '

When Scott rapped at the open door a

minute or so later, Mitch and Agnes were so startled that they sprang apart as if they'd been caught doing something wrong.

Seeing as much, Scott gave a rare faintly mocking smile. 'I'm going out to look for Diana,' he said.

'Good idea,' Agnes said. 'Maybe the serenity of the desert will take your mind off the *real* reason you're here.'

'What're you talking about?'

'Oh, don't bother trying to deny it, Scott. I always could read you like a book.'

He glanced meaningfully at Mitch, uncomfortable with the prospect of discussing the subject in front of someone he considered to be an outsider. 'I'm not giving up,' he warned. 'I'll *never* give up. One third of that gold is mine, and with or without your help, I intend to get it!'

Mitch said: 'Maybe I should leave you two . . . '

'No,' Agnes said quickly. 'No, don't leave, Mitch. You've heard the talk. You know there's nothing to it.'

Scott threw him a withering look, then

stalked to the door. As he reached it, Mitch called impulsively, 'Scott?'

'Yes?'

'Mind if I tag along?'

Scott made no attempt to hide his surprise.

'It'd give us a chance to talk. You know, get to know each other better.'

Scott considered it and finally shrugged. 'Why not? I guess two pairs of eyes are better than one.'

They left the room together.

* * *

They drove in silence for a while. Around them the furnace-hot desert stretched to all points of the compass, a hostile environment that had a disturbing tendency to chew up the unwary and spit them out in little, deep-fried pieces.

Finally Mitch said: 'Couple of months.'

Scott, pretending to concentrate on his driving, blinked. 'Excuse me?'

'Weren't you getting ready to ask me how long I've known your sister?'

Scott reddened.

'And now you're wondering why she didn't say anything about me when you called a few days ago, right?'

Scott shrugged. 'The thought *did* cross my mind.'

'It's because she wanted to surprise you,' Mitch said. 'And by the way your mouth dropped when you met me, I'd say she scored big.' Enjoying the other man's discomfort, he added: 'Go ahead. Keep pumping me.'

Scott kept his eyes on the trail ahead. 'No need to get pissy about it. Wouldn't *you* want to know all about the guy who was marrying *your* sister?'

'I guess. If I had a sister. And if the dude in question was an out-of-work trucker who'd read all about her old man hitting paydirt . . . '

Scott floored the brake, brought the Camaro to a slithering halt. 'I knew it! You sonofabitch! You don't love Agnes. You're after Dad's gold!'

'So?' said Mitch. 'That makes two of us, right?'

Scott shook his head, enraged. 'At least I'm entitled to it.'

'I got no argument with that.'

It was the last thing he'd been expecting to hear. Scott studied him curiously for a moment, while disturbed dust settled slowly around them.

'Are you offering to cut me in?'

'What do you think?'

'My God, you must be pretty sure of yourself to take a risk like that. What if I — '

' — told Agnes?' Mitch finished. 'Go ahead. You think she hates you now, you try ruining her fantasy by telling her that the guy she loves is conning her. She'll spit in your face and have me toss you out on your prissy little ass!'

To add some weight to the threat, he leaned forward threateningly, causing Scott to shrink back.

'You don't have to go all primitive on me,' he said.

Mitch only grinned at him. 'Oh, I bet you'd *like* for me to go primitive on you, though, wouldn't you?'

He reached over and stroked Scott's cheek softly. Scott flinched, but didn't pull away.

'How about it, cutie?' Mitch asked. 'Am I right?'

'I . . . I don't know what you mean.'

'Sure you do,' chuckled Mitch. 'I've seen the way you look at me. Same way your wife looks at me, and we both know what *she* wants.'

Scott licked his suddenly-dry lips. Hesitantly, his heart pounding, he asked, 'What if I, uh . . . were interested in you? Would that make a difference?'

'Only if you know where the gold's buried.' Mitch dropped his hand to Scott's knee, squeezed gently. 'Then I'd say let's dig it up tonight and blast out of here. Just you and me.'

Scott shifted nervously to accommodate his growing erection. 'What about Agnes?'

Behind his Aviators, Mitch's blue eyes took on a languid, lazy quality. 'She can keep Kelly-Anne company,' he said softly.

Scott's mouth dropped open. 'You mean dump . . . ?' He couldn't stifle the short, high giggle that came to his lips. 'Oh God,' he said. 'Kell' would be so pissed.'

'Which would bother you for all of what — one fucking second?'

Captivated by the idea Scott nodded absently. 'She deserves it, the bitch.'

'So why did you marry her?'

Scott looked at him, then quickly glanced away.

Mitch frowned, suddenly caught on and said: 'Wait a minute! You guys aren't married! She's just a beard.' He whistled. 'Sonofabitch! Agnes was right — the only reason you're here is to get the gold!'

Finding a little backbone, Scott said: 'One way or another.'

'So give,' said Mitch. 'Where's it buried?'

'You think I'd be driving around in this hell-hole, looking for Diana, if I already *knew*?'

'It's Diana who knows, then?'

Scott nodded.

'But she wouldn't tell you?'

'Not over the phone. She just told me to make sure Agnes didn't suspect why I was coming.'

'So you invented a wife,' Mitch mused with a slow smile. 'Not bad. How much is

Kelly-Anne in for?'

'Half. But — '

'I know,' grinned Mitch. 'You'll, ah, 'mail her share to her,' right?'

Scott's return grin told him that they understood each other perfectly.

'All right,' said Mitch, leaning back. 'We've got everything to play for, you and me. So let's keep looking. It'll be dark soon.'

★   ★   ★

Benji snuck into the house through the open back door and padded through the kitchen, and out into the hallway. Tightening his jaws around his latest prize, he ascended the stairs in a noiseless blur, paused at the top and then considered his next move.

He slunk along to the door of the room in which his mistress's brother and the other woman were staying, nosed it open and slipped inside.

The room was empty. But Benji heard the sound of running water coming from the connecting bathroom, the high, indistinct sound of the woman in there, singing to herself.

Benji crossed to the open bathroom door, set his prize down, studied the naked shape behind the shower curtain impassively.

The woman was soaping herself vigorously, running her open palms down across her breasts, over her belly, up into her armpits, then turning to allow the shower to rinse her clean.

Benji picked up his prize again and entered the bathroom, leapt silently onto the laundry basket, then up again onto the high window sill. He slunk along to the end of the sill and finally jumped up onto the dull silver shower rail. He made no more noise than a thought.

He looked down at the woman. Her wet red hair hung down between her shoulder blades like so many glistening worms. Soap, driven by the hot, needling water from the shower head, slid over and between her breasts, dripped from her nipples, continued on down her hips and thighs to puddle at her feet.

Her eyes were closed, and there was a

half-smile on her face. She was enjoying the shower. Just as she would no doubt enjoy Benji's prize.

But for Kelly-Anne just then the *real* prize was still beyond her reach. Although she had made numerous attempts to engage Agnes in conversation in order to judge her mental health and find some way in which Scott might legitimately take control of the Shelby estate, Agnes simply wasn't cooperating. No matter the question, her answers were always vague or, worse still from Scott's point of view, completely normal. It was true that she had insecurity issues, issues with her self-esteem and clearly displayed the symptoms of OCD. But was she crazy?

Kelly-Anne honestly couldn't say.

She did get the uneasy feeling that Agnes knew exactly what she was up to, however, and that meant that she would have to tread even more carefully from now on. She suspected that Agnes had seen through their little deception, realised that she and Scott weren't married, wondered why Scott had brought her along for the ride and, based on the kind of seemingly innocuous questions Kelly had been asking, eventually put two and two together. It was possible. Certainly Agnes was bright enough to have made such a connection.

At length Kelly-Anne reached out blindly to switch off the shower. Steam rose slowly toward the ceiling. She screwed up her face to squeeze the water from around her eyes, opened them at last and looked down at her body, at the soapy water swirling away down the drain.

At the water . . .

. . . and the blood dripping into it.

Blood?

Kelly-Anne felt a sudden stab of panic. Bleeding?

She was *bleeding?*

In the next instant something wet and heavy smacked against her bare feet and then rolled lazily onto the shower floor, splashing blood and water across her shins.

It was a half-chewed rat.

A big, black rat curled in on itself, its long, thick tail stiff as a pencil.

She felt bile rise in her throat.

Its snout had been chewed off. Something had torn at its soft belly, exposing its pink innards. Its claws met just below its missing jaw, almost as if it had died midway through a prayer.

Kelly Anne jumped away from it, a scream building in her throat. She backed up against the wet shower curtain: cold now, it stuck to her back and butt like a shroud.

She saw something move from the corner of her eye and her head snapped up.

A slate-grey cat with silver-tipped fur was hunched over the shower rail. The minute their eyes met, it opened its mouth and chirruped at her; and in that moment any cute or homely quality that it might otherwise have possessed was replaced by something wilder, darker, more feral.

A second later the cat threw itself off the rail, landed noiselessly on the bathroom floor and vanished.

And that was when Kelly-Anne finally screamed.

When Agnes came running, she found
Kelly-Anne in the shower, staring down
at the dead rat in a state of near hysteria.

She slapped Kelly-Anne's face harder
than she really needed to, but the slap
had the desired effect: it brought her back
to her senses, and then Agnes was able to
lead her from the shower stall, snatch up
a towel and drape it around Kelly-Anne's
shoulders before guiding her out into the
bedroom.

She closed the bathroom door behind
her, pushed Kelly-Anne down onto the
edge of the nearest bed and towelled her
neck and shoulders briskly.

'What happened?' she asked. 'Where
did that rat come from?'

Kelly-Anne was shivering, and beneath
her tan she looked pale. Her perfect
hazel-gold eyes held a vaguely glazed
look. She was scared out of her wits.

Agnes, by contrast, was cool, calm and
collected, and the knowledge gave her a
tremendous feeling of strength and
power.

'Stay here,' she said, 'and dry yourself off.'

Kelly-Annie looked up at her. 'I — '

'I'll be right back,' Agnes assured her.

She was as good as her word. When she came back, she was holding a glass of Bushmills. Kelly-Anne snatched the glass and drained half of its contents in one gulp. She shuddered, coughed a bit, but it seemed to complete her recovery, and after that she was able to tell Agnes what had happened.

Even before the last words had left her lips, however, Agnes was shaking her head. 'You must be mistaken. In all the years I've had Benji, he's never brought a single dead animal into the house.'

'Well, it didn't just crawl up on top of the shower by itself,' snapped Kelly-Anne.

'No, no, of course not,' said Agnes. 'But are you *sure* you saw Benji?'

'I saw a cat,' Kelly-Anne said. 'Grey. Orange eyes. Evil-looking. Then it disappeared.'

Agnes appeared to give the description some thought. 'It could have been one of the feral cats we get hereabouts,' she suggested.

In no mood for conjecture, Kelly-Anne waved that away. 'God,' she whispered, 'I hate rats, as well.'

Agnes nodded sympathetically.

'Yes,' she said, almost dreamily. 'So do I. They live in the walls, you know. Sometimes I hear them at night. Gnawing . . . '

★　★　★

As soon as Mitch and Scott got back to the house, Kelly-Anne told them what had happened to her in the shower. To her great irritation, however, both men seemed to be more concerned just then with Diana's continued absence.

'We drove around for hours,' said Mitch, addressing Agnes. 'Saw every freakin' creature that desert's got to offer . . . except Diana.'

Scott's growing disquiet was equally obvious. 'It's like she's vanished off the face of the earth.'

Agnes tilted her head sympathetically to him. 'You mustn't worry about her,' she advised. 'This is nothing new, remember. Sometimes she disappears for days at a time.'

'Well,' he replied firmly, 'I'm going out again tomorrow — and this time I'm going to *find* her.'

Later, while Agnes was re-taping his ankle for him, Mitch told her all about his earlier conversation with Scott. 'I can't believe you didn't know he was gay,' he grinned at the finish. 'Jeez, didn't you even get a hint?'

'Well, I knew he was a little . . . feminine,' she allowed. 'If that's what you mean. But I always blamed that on Momma's pampering. She never let him get dirty or play with other boys. It wasn't easy for him.'

She sat back on her calves, the job done. 'How's that?' she asked.

He stood up and carefully put a little weight on the injury. 'Good,' he said after a moment. 'I can almost walk on it.'

He flopped back onto the edge of the bed. 'Well, be glad he *is* gay,' he said, returning to the subject of Scott. 'Otherwise, he never would have taken the bait. At least now we know for sure why he's here, and that Diana knows where the gold's buried.'

She gave him a strange look.

'What?' he asked. 'You still don't believe there *is* any?'

'I don't know what to believe,' Agnes replied. 'But even if there is, how would *she* know where it is? Papa wouldn't have told her. Certainly not before telling me.'

'Well, *somebody* told her,' Mitch insisted. 'Or else she spied on him while he was burying it.'

'Papa couldn't have buried it,' she argued. 'His arthritis was so bad by then that he couldn't even light his pipe.'

'Then he must've had help,' Mitch decided. 'And that was the person who told her.'

9

As soon as Agnes went to bed, Mitch put his boot back on, grabbed the crutch and quit his room. Around him, the house was quiet. Kelly-Anne, still shaken by her earlier encounter with the cat, had gone to bed early, while Scott had elected to settle in the den with a bottle of Bushmills and brood over Diana's whereabouts.

He descended the stairs as quietly as possible, let himself out into the night and closed the front door softly behind him.

Still limping but definitely on the mend, he followed the hardpan track up the hill toward the snake-farm.

Something followed him.

Long before he reached the diner, he thought he heard the high, distinctive chirrup of Agnes's cat in the darkness. He paused to listen more carefully and then frowned. No . . . no, there was a more . . . musical quality to this sound.

If he didn't know better, he'd swear that someone somewhere was playing a flute.

As he closed on the diner, the sound grew a little clearer. He peered into the building through one of the broken windows, but the only patrons there tonight were shadows.

He let himself in through the glassless door and tip-toed across the tiled floor, crunching dust underfoot. Then he skirted around what was left of the counter and through the door into the darkened kitchen beyond. At the far end of the kitchen — which, just like the rest of the place, had been more or less gutted — he saw a bar of light showing beneath the storeroom door and crept closer. The lilting flute music grew louder.

He reached out, took hold of the door handle and turned it.

It was hard to describe what he saw inside.

The walls were covered in garish neon signs. They stretched from skirting to ceiling, all their wires leading to one overcrowded multi-socket beside the portable TV. One sign read *MASONIC TEMPLE*, another *AZTEC BOWLING*. There were signs advertising *COCKTAILS, GOOD FOOD, 24-HOUR LIQUOR, DELI, COFFEE* and *SHOE REPAIRS*. Some were lit up, others buzzed and flickered on and off. They were the room's only light source, and as a consequence, the room itself appeared almost to glow.

Mitch looked around in a mixture of surprise and disbelief. Nothing could have prepared him for this. But at least he now knew how Neon had come by his name.

The man himself was sitting on an old futon along the right-side wall, wearing jeans and a stained undershirt. He'd been playing a long, homemade bamboo flute until the door opened. Now he sat like a statue, the flute still held close to his pursed lips, his stubby fingers still poised over the holes, but temporarily forgotten.

He looked up at Mitch through nervous eyes.

Mitch said, 'Man, it must've taken years to collect all this stuff.'

Neon shrugged. 'Started when I was a

kid in the projects,' he replied. 'Ever' time they tore down an old buildin', I'd steal the neon from it.'

He hesitated a moment, then thrust his chin in the general direction of the aging Westinghouse refrigerator in the opposite corner. 'If you want a Bud, help yourself.'

'Thanks.'

While he did just that, Neon started playing the flute again. Under his guidance it made an aimless, mournful sound. Mitch tried to pick out the tune but it didn't seem to have one.

'We got to talk, bro',' he said after opening the bottle and taking a pull.

Neon took the instrument away from his whiskery lips again. 'What about?' he asked softly.

'Gold,' Mitch replied.

Neon gave his head a rapid shake. 'I don' know nothin' 'bout no gold.'

He was about to put the flute back to his lips when Mitch moved across to an old red-and-white *COCA-COLA* sign that looked as if it dated back to the forties. He tapped it gently with the bottle.

'This looks pretty fragile,' he noted, almost to himself.

Hurriedly, Neon sat forward. 'Hey, man, don't do that!'

Mitch studied the sign some more. 'Breaks real easy, I bet. 'Specially after so many years.'

Neon set the flute aside and stood up. He came no higher than Mitch's shoulder. 'What you want from me, man?' he asked, his voice taking on a whine. 'I don't know where — '

'Save it,' snapped Mitch. 'You've been here for years, Neon. You've *got* to know. You probably even helped ol' Flapjack bury the stuff.'

Neon gave his head another hurried shake and turned away from him. 'Tha's crazy! You think I'd hang around a dump like this if I knew where — '

Mitch whacked the *COCA-COLA* sign, and it didn't so much break apart as disintegrate. As bits of brittle plastic, light strip and dust feathered to the floor, Neon watched through bug eyes, looking like he might bust an artery at any moment.

'Aw, shit, man! Don't do that!'

Mitch eyed him coldly. 'You know how to stop me,' he replied.

He moved on to the next sign, which read *STANLEY MEYER JEWELLERS*. He drew back his free arm as if preparing to give this sign the same treatment he'd accorded to the previous one. Neon didn't think he could stand to witness something like that again, and his chestnut face scrunched up.

'Wait!' he cried. 'Okay, okay . . . '

Mitch turned and gave him a cool grin. 'That's more like it,' he said. 'All right — give.'

'I don't know where any gold is,' Neon said in a rush. 'But one night, years ago, I helped Mr Shelby load a big chest onto his truck.'

'Go on.'

'Well, tha's it.'

'The hell it is. What was in it?'

'I never ast and he never said.'

'Any idea where he took it?'

When Neon made no immediate reply, Mitch turned and started to inspect the *STANLEY MEYER* sign again. Neon said quickly, 'Last I saw, he was drivin' up the slope toward those rocks. You know them rocks, where the girls' pets're buried?'

'I know 'em,' said Mitch. Reaching a quick decision he said, 'We're gonna need shovels.'

Neon said, 'We got shovels in the tool shed out back.'

'All right. Let's go.'

The handyman's rheumy eyes bugged. '*Now?*'

'Now.'

'But — '

'Just get your frigging jacket and stop arguing!'

With no real say in the matter, Neon grabbed his coat and they left the room, crunched back through the darkened diner and out into the cool night. From there, Mitch followed his reluctant companion around to the back of the building, where Neon had parked his VW beside Flapjack Shelby's tarp-covered pickup.

'You' crazy, you know that?' the black man muttered. 'This ain't the place to go pokin' around in, 'specially after dark!'

'Afraid of ghosts?' asked Mitch.

'The dead're dead,' Neon replied. 'But you got to watch yourself in these parts, Mr Akins. Much as anythin' else, they's sinkholes ever'where.'

'Sinkholes?'

'Yeah. You know. Like the ground's not as solid as it looks.'

'I know what a sinkhole is. I just didn't think you had any around here.'

'Oh, sure. These slopes, the desert out yonder, it's riddled with 'em. Water table hereabouts gets lower ever' year, see, an' as it drops it undermines the ground. Tha's why the Highway Commission built the new interstate three miles away.'

A cool wind sprang up and Mitch suppressed a shiver. He hated the desert and the way it had of making you feel like you were being watched all the time.

The tool shed sat just the other side of the parked cars. Neon unlocked and opened the weathered door. It creaked dryly, and as it did so Mitch thought he heard the lonely chirrup of a cat in the surrounding darkness and immediately threw an uneasy glance over one shoulder.

Neon disappeared inside, made a few

sporadic sounds clattering around in the darkness. His nerves already stretched tight, Mitch thought he heard another sound, a soft *shushing* coming from someplace behind him. He turned fast and could've sworn he caught a fleeting glimpse of . . . *something*, moving from one patch of cover to another, about thirty, forty feet away.

Then Neon shuffled out again, carrying a shovel in each gnarled hand. As he held one out to Mitch he said worriedly, 'Miss Agnes ain't gonna like this . . . '

'You let me worry about — '

That was as far as he got.

In the same moment he saw Neon's pouchy eyes widen in fear, he heard another soft sound behind him. Instinctively he threw himself to one side even as something hurtled past him, whacked Neon hard in the chest and slammed him back against the open shed door.

As the shovels fell from his hands, Neon tore the darkness apart with a startled yelp that quickly trailed off into a wet gurgle, and Mitch, rolling now, trying to get into cover behind the cars, thought something jumbled and crazy, like *jesus-christ-what-the-fuck*.

At last he came up on his knees beside the parked truck, scuttled into cover behind it and stared off into the darkness.

The night appeared quiet, calm, empty.

'Neon!' Mitch whispered without taking his eyes off the surrounding desert. 'Neon, you okay?'

There came no reply.

'Neon?'

He heard something then, something barely audible that made his skin crawl.

It was a sob.

He stared into the darkness for maybe half a minute more, until he was reasonably sure that whoever had been out there was long gone. Only then did he dare break cover and limp around to the front of the tool shed.

He whispered, 'Aw Christ . . .'

He could hardly take in what had happened.

Neon had been skewered through the chest with a pitchfork. It had struck him with such force that the forks themselves had gone right through and pinned him to the shed door behind him. Blood still oozed from around each of the four rusted tines, glistening wetly in the moonlight. The little man's chest was covered in it.

And yet, incredibly, he was still alive.

Mitch took a horrified step away from him, thinking, *Aw man . . .*

Hearing the movement, Neon raised his head sluggishly, looked at him without really seeing him at all. His bloodied lips worked for a moment, and then the life drained from his rheumy eyes and his head slumped forward, chin on chest.

Mitch said, 'No . . . ' and shook his head a few times, but the blood didn't go away, the pitchfork didn't go away, Neon didn't come back to life.

This nightmare was real.

And then, all at once —

— a soft chirruping sound drifted in out of the surrounding shadows.

His temper flaring, Mitch turned, folded his fists, yelled, 'Show yourself, goddammit!'

There came no response. The chirruping drifted away, and somewhere far off a

165

coyote howled his mournful howl.

All at once Mitch felt like he was going to pass out. He muttered, 'Christ,' again, and wondered just what the fuck he'd gotten himself involved in.

★ ★ ★

'And this sound you say you keep hearing,' said Mel Crane, looking up from his notes, 'it's definitely a cat's meow?'

It was a little after dawn the following morning, and already it was shaping up to be another hot one.

Mitch nodded. 'Yeah. Not so much a meow, more like a kind of chirrup. But definitely a cat.'

Crane remembered the sound he'd heard up at the snake-farm the previous day. Chirrup was a good word to describe it. 'And the first time you heard it was when? Night before last?'

'Yeah. When Aggie asked me to check outside to make sure the burglar wasn't still hanging around.'

The sheriff made a note of that.

After replacing the shovels in the tool

shed, Mitch had returned to the house and spun a hurried story about having gone out to make one last quick search for Diana before turning in, then hearing a scream and finding Neon pinned to the tool shed door.

Scott had recovered from the shock first, at least enough to fix him a drink and tell him to *sit* down and then *calm* down. Agnes had joined them shortly afterward. And shortly after that, she'd called the police department.

Sheriff Crane turned up a couple of hours later, followed by a mobile crime lab, a police photographer and a sombre, spectacle-wearing man from the Medical Examiner's office. The crime scene itself was sealed off with yellow tape and the CSI people set to work. Neon was examined by the M.E., the pitchfork was dusted for fingerprints and finally removed from the body, to be bagged, tagged and placed on the back seat of Crane's Tahoe. Neon himself was zipped into a body bag and taken away in a black ambulance.

Now Crane and Mitch stood within sight of the shed, Mitch still having a hard time trying to tear his eyes away from the dark patch of dried blood that marked the spot to which Neon had been pinned.

The sheriff put his notebook and pencil away, then produced a kerchief with which he blotted his hands clean. Only then did he carefully remove his beloved Stetson and wipe his brow.

'Why don't you just go out and buy another hat?' asked Mitch, suddenly growing short on patience. 'Something cheap you could wear all the time without giving a damn what happens to it?'

'I tried that once,' Crane replied soberly. 'But it felt like I'd spent a day without Mabel at my side.' He offered a short smile, then said, 'You think this is all my fault, don't you, Mr Akins? That if I'd done my job and collared Miss Agnes's burglar right away, Neon would still be alive?'

Without making any attempt to sound sincere, Mitch said, 'I'm sure you're doing everything you can.'

'I'm glad to hear it,' replied the sheriff. 'Because I don't for one minute think that your, ah, burglar, killed Neon.'

Mitch frowned at him. 'Why not? Don't tell me. This is one of those 'gut feelings' you've learned to trust, right?'

Crane eyed him for a long moment. 'You're a needling sonofabitch, aren't you?' he said bluntly.

'I'll take that as a yes,' said Mitch.

'Burglars have M.O.s, just like any other criminals,' stated Crane. 'They don't tend to hang around after a robbery.'

'Unless maybe they've got a reason.'

'The gold, you mean?' asked Crane. Relishing the look of surprise his comment evoked, he said, 'Everyone around here knows about it, son — including you.'

Mitch blinked. 'Jesus, you think *I* killed Neon?'

'The thought *did* cross my mind.'

'Aw, come on, now! Why would I want to — '

He stopped suddenly, catching something in Crane's dark eyes.

'You're messing with me, aren't you?' he said softly.

Crane nodded. 'Just wanted you to

know that you don't have the monopoly on needling, son.'

He turned and retraced his steps down toward the house and his car. Scott and Kelly-Anne were waiting anxiously beside the vehicle. Agnes was standing just inside the front doorway, watching as they came back down the slope.

When they were near enough, Scott called, 'All done here, sheriff?'

'For the moment,' Crane replied. As if it had just occurred to him, he suddenly reached into the Tahoe and drew out the plastic-wrapped pitchfork. 'One last question, though. Before I turn this over to the crime lab, any of you care to hazard a guess at what *this* is?'

He pointed to a small, brownish stain on the handle. It measured maybe three inches square and had blurred edges.

'Dried blood?' said Scott.

'That's what I thought,' said Crane. 'At first. But dried blood crumbles like caked mud. This has a kind of . . . greasy . . . texture to it.'

'How about shoe polish?' suggested Kelly-Anne. 'Or make-up.'

Crane treated her to a nod of approval. 'Now you see why I was all for women joining the department. They bring a whole new perspective to things.'

He put the pitchfork back in the car, climbed in after it, and promising to come back later, gunned the engine and drove off.

Mitch turned and limped back to the house. Kelly-Anne, still watching the sheriff drive away, said to Scott, 'Am I crazy, or did he just imply that the killer is a woman?'

Lost in thought, Scott started to his Camaro. 'Come on.'

'Where are we going?'

'To look for Diana.'

Kelly-Anne frowned. 'You heard what Agnes said. She'll come home when she's ready.'

'I'm sure she would,' he said. 'Under normal circumstances. But these *aren't* normal circumstances, are they?'

'You can say that again.'

'If you don't want to go, I'll go alone.'

'Like hell you will. I just don't see why we have to go at all.'

171

'There's a killer out there somewhere,' he said. 'Let's just hope we find Diana before *he* does.'

Remembering what Sheriff Crane had just implied, she added, 'Or *she*.'

10

As soon as Scott's car vanished over the rise, Mitch grabbed Agnes by the arm and more or less dragged her into the den.

'Mitch!' she complained, dragging her heels a little in protest. 'You're hurting me!'

'I'm sorry,' he said tightly. 'But we're running out of time here, Aggie.'

She frowned. 'Run — ? I don't understand.'

As patiently as he could, he said, 'I don't know how much longer you can protect Diana.'

She suddenly went very still.

'What do you mean?' she asked after a long pause.

Mitch sighed and threw a glance at the sun-filled four-window bay. 'That sheriff's not as dumb as he looks. I think he suspects that Diana killed Neon.'

Agnes swayed. 'No!'

'He'd suspect you too,' he continued. 'But he's probably guessed by now that you're agoraphobic.'

Agnes's frown deepened and she made a disdainful, dismissive sound in her throat. 'What are you talking about? I can leave any — '

'Ah, Aggie, cut the crap!' he interrupted tiredly. 'Crane's not the only one who pretends to be dumb. I saw it for myself the first night I met you. You wouldn't even set foot across that threshold for your precious cat!'

She sagged as some of the fight went out of her. 'Why did you bother to come back, then?' she asked miserably.

'We made a deal,' he reminded her. 'And when I make a deal, I stick to it.'

Grabbing her by the shoulders, he went on tightly, 'Diana's in deep shit, Aggie, and right now I think I'm the only one who can get her out of it. But first you've got to tell me where she's hiding, 'cause when the sheriff gets back, he'll be fetching a posse with him, and as desert-savvy as Diana is, she won't be able to hide from helicopters, deputies and satellites that can see you spitting on a sidewalk! Aggie, she won't last a fucking *second.*'

Agnes's lower lip quivered. She crossed the room to the mantel, looked up at Diana's portrait and half-whispered, 'Oh God, what have I done?'

'It's a little late for tears and violins,' he told her harshly. 'You knew all along that she was dangerous. That's *really* why you couldn't leave here even when your father's business went down the toilet. You couldn't risk letting her roam around in the big city. You'd be turning loose a serial killer.'

She turned, came back and buried her face in his chest, the words pouring out of her in a desperate babble. 'Oh, Mitch, you don't know how hard it's been to keep people from finding out . . . '

'I'm sure Neon appreciated that,' he remarked.

She pushed back, looked up at him, her expression desperate. 'Mitch, I swear I never thought he was in any danger. Diana always seemed so . . . fond of him.'

'Oh, sure,' he cut back. 'You could

almost say she loved him to death. Well, now you've got a choice. I can try to bring her in safe and sound, or you can let the law do it. But if you wait for the law, and she resists arrest, the chances are that she won't make it back alive.'

★ ★ ★

Kelly-Anne would have said that Scott stopped the car in the middle of nowhere, except for the fact that as far as she was concerned this entire Godforsaken desert was the middle of nowhere.

They'd been driving for perhaps thirty minutes, with Scott trying his best to quarter the desert in some sort of order. When the trail — and she used the term loosely — eventually led them to a broken ridge, he cut the engine and got out in order to take a closer look at what lay on the far side.

The short answer to that was more desert, of course. As Kelly-Anne climbed out behind him, the full heat of the morning struck her like a blow, and she wilted almost immediately.

Scott, meanwhile, began to descend the slope in long strides, pushing loose sand ahead of him in sluggish, rippling waves.

'Diana!' he cried. 'Diana, it's Scottie! Can you hear me? We need to talk!'

He stopped and looked around, waiting for a reply that never came. At length he struggled back up to the ridge, his shirt soaked with sweat.

'It just doesn't make any sense,' he muttered once he'd caught his breath. 'Why tell me to come all the way out here only to pull a vanishing act?'

Kelly-Anne shrugged. 'Change of heart?'

'Then why not say that to my face?'

'Who knows? Maybe she doesn't like confrontation. Or maybe she just decided to keep all that gold for herself.'

Scott shook his head adamantly. 'If you knew Diana, you wouldn't say that. She's wild, yes. Unpredictable, yes. But greedy? No way.'

'Well, whatever the reason, let's call it quits,' she said. 'We've checked everywhere you thought she might be, and I'm on the verge of a total meltdown.'

Scott studied her momentarily. 'Are

you saying we should give this up? Just turn our backs on a fortune?'

'I don't know what else there is to try,' she replied. 'And we still don't really know for sure that there's any fortune to turn our backs on.'

He ran a forearm across his brow. 'Look, we're not far from the Old Back Road now. That's the place she *always* comes to, sooner or later. She came here after Momma died and she's been coming back ever since. If she's around here anywhere, it'll be there.'

'The Old Back Road,' she repeated. 'Didn't Neon say he drove by there on his way back from town? He said she wasn't there.'

'Just because he didn't see her doesn't mean she wasn't there,' he replied. 'What say we go there now and take one final look around? If we still can't find her after that, we'll go back. All right?'

'All right,' she said grudgingly.

They got back in the car and after pausing briefly to check his bearings, Scott tooled the Camaro back onto the main trail and headed south.

About twenty minutes later they came to a rutted trail that dipped towards and then curved between two slanting sandstone walls that shouldered up to the cloudless azure sky. The low brush that carpeted both slopes was stippled here and there with patches of orange-tipped prickly pear, milkweed and rose-wood, but for all that Kelly-Anne still felt that the canyon had about it a curiously hushed, lifeless quality.

Scott kept the Camaro bouncing and bunny-hopping over the rough track for another mile, then finally brought the vehicle to a halt.

'All right,' he said as they climbed out into the hot sunlight. 'We'll split up and each see what we can find. You check the slopes and caves back the way we've just come, I'll check everything further north. Give it thirty minutes and then we'll meet back here, okay?'

She eyed him sceptically. 'I don't think it's such a good idea to split up.'

'We'll cover twice the ground in half the time,' he reasoned. 'And you never know, one of us might get lucky.'

179

She considered the prospect for a few seconds, then reluctantly agreed. 'But I'm not going far,' she added.

'Just do what you can,' he said, and started off along the canyon floor.

Kelly-Anne watched him go. She then grudgingly set off in the opposite direction, climbing awkwardly in her figure-hugging designer jeans and Loeffler Randall ballet flats.

As she climbed she grew hot and irritable. She was an intelligent woman, level-headed, sensible and focused, so why had she ever allowed someone like Scott Shelby to talk her into participating in such a ridiculous charade?

The answer was, of course, greed. And she knew that whatever else she might be, she was and always would be totally, incurably greedy.

She blamed her parents for that. Her father was a successful property developer, her mother a psychologist. Born to wealth, Kelly-Anne herself had been educated at exclusive schools in California, New York and Connecticut. Growing up, she'd spent her winters skiing in

Aspen and her summers building a tan in the Caribbean. For Kelly-Anne, there had never been any such thing as *enough*.

But all that changed when she left med school and went out into the world as a residency-graduate. No longer able to live off the generous allowance her parents had previously made available to her, instead receiving on-the-job training for a fraction of the salary she could eventually expect to earn, Kelly-Anne had tasted hardship — *her* idea of hardship, at least — for the very first time, and had despised it. In fact, the experience had coloured her entire outlook on life, and once it was over she'd promised herself that never again would she ever take less than she could get.

All of which meant that she now had only herself to blame. Greed was her major failing. She knew that. But the rich and powerful could afford such failings, and Kelly-Anne intended to be both before she grew much older.

Carefully she climbed higher, occasionally stopping to push the hair back off her face and scan her surroundings for any signs of life. Around her the ragged canyon walls were pocked and scarred by the passage of aeons. Everything was still and silent save for the occasional screech of a red tail hawk.

Here and there she saw splits in the rock: the slim entrances to caves where Diana might have decided to hide. But if Scott expected her to investigate those, he could think again. Kelly-Anne was going to do just enough and no more.

She made it to a level rocky shelf covered with sun-bleached brush, checked the area for snakes and spiders then flopped down. Sweat darkened the back of her sleeveless brown top and with a grimace she peeled it away from her back.

It was then she heard a low, ominous chirruping sound above and to her left.

Scrambling to her feet, she looked towards the sound and shielded her eyes from the bright sunlight. She thought she saw something small and dark crouching on the ridge above her but couldn't be certain.

In the next moment the shape leaped at her.

It was Benji, claws extended, lips drawn back in an angry snarl. The cat landed on her left shoulder and dug his claws into Kelly-Anne's coppery flesh.

Startled, she tried to protect herself with her arms, at the same time back-pedalling and trying to drag him off her. Benji clawed wildly at her and sank his fangs into her hand.

Crying out in pain, she jumped back and stumbled over a rock. Her ankle twisted. She gasped, lost her balance and went down hard. Instantly, the cat went for her face, raking her cheek with its claws.

The pain was almost unbearable.

Kelly-Anne screamed, managed to get a grip on the cat and flung it away from her. Benji landed on all fours, arched his back and again hurled himself at her. He went for her face. Screaming, she ripped the cat from her, its claws and teeth leaving long bloody scratches.

She flung him away, hoping he would break his back against a rock. But again he landed on all fours and disappeared into the undergrowth.

Sobbing with pain, Kelly-Anne sat there shaking, blood running from the scratches on her face and hands. Dazed and in shock, she dragged herself up. Pain shot up from her twisted ankle. Gritting her teeth, she stumbled unsteadily down off the ledge and headed back for the car.

★ ★ ★

Agnes fetched a sheet of paper, spread it out on the beech wood table and sketched out a rough map of the area.

'This is the Old Back Road,' she explained while Mitch studied the drawing over her shoulder. 'It's where Diana always goes to hide.'

She next drew a series of crosses along the length of what was supposed to be the cliffs overlooking the road. These, she said, were the approximate positions of the caves where Diana might seek shelter.

'Promise me you won't hurt her,' she said, handing him the map.

He tucked it into his shirt pocket. 'I'll do what I can, Agnes. But if she tries to kill me like she killed Neon . . . well, I won't roll over and go quietly.'

'I wouldn't want you to, sweetheart.' She cupped her hands about his face and kissed him fondly but clumsily on the lips. 'I'd die if anything happened to you.'

'Nothing's gonna happen,' he promised. 'To me *or* your sister. Once she knows what her options are, she'd be nuts not to give up.'

But then again, he reminded himself, *she's nuts anyway.*

He headed for the door and let himself out. Agnes followed him as far as the doorframe, but no farther.

'Don't forget,' he said. 'If the sheriff shows up, stall him. It could be dark by the time I get back, and I don't want to get shot by some trigger-happy deputy.'

She nodded. 'Be careful.'

He turned and hop-walked up the rise to the back of the gas station, where Neon's ugly little yellow VW Beetle sat baking in the sun. It was already a little past noon and all that was left of the police presence now was a length of crime scene tape, fluttering in the light breeze.

As he vanished over the rise, Agnes

closed the door with a sigh and slowly climbed the stairs to her room. It was hot and she was tired almost beyond belief. Diana's disappearance, Scott's arrival, Kelly-Anne's constant probing questions and Neon's murder . . . each incident had taken its toll on her already fragile nerves. The only silver lining had been Mitch, coming into her life the way he had.

She went into her room, on into the connecting bathroom and peeled off her white gloves. She was rinsing her hands under cold water when a figure appeared silently behind her.

'You had your chance,' said Diana.

Startled, Agnes looked into the mirror. Behind her tinted glasses her eyes grew wide when she saw who was sharing the reflection with her.

Looking more feral than ever, Diana said, 'Now he's *mine*.'

* * *

Mitch followed Aggie's directions as best he could, but he was soon lost. After twenty minutes he killed the engine and climbed out of the VW. Studying the map again, he tried to link it up with any likely-looking landmarks.

After a while he took off his cap, sleeved the sweat from his forehead and then spat off to one side. *You've screwed up, babe*, he thought. *You've sent me the long way round.*

He shook his head, climbed back into the Beetle and drove on. It was late afternoon, and coming on for dusk when he finally found the Old Back Road and followed it into the canyon Agnes had drawn.

It was a timeless place, with steep, seamed walls the colour of mustard. He followed the road for about half a mile, then stopped and tried to match the scattered caves in the cliffs with the crosses Agnes had drawn on the map.

At length he got out of the car and called Diana's name. His only replies were echoes.

'Diana, it's me, Mitch! Agnes sent me out to talk to you!'

The echoes faded.

'Listen! It's important! It's about

Neon! The sheriff knows you killed him!'

He fell silent then, watching, waiting.

At first there was no response.

Then, at last, a small rock came bouncing down the cliff wall and hit the ground close to the VW's fender.

He swallowed.

She was up there, then.

And she could hear him.

Another rock followed the first. It flew out from the ridge, coal-black against the viridian streaks and magenta swirls of the darkening sky. It hit the dirt a little closer to the VW and then bounced away.

Mitch moved around behind the car.

'I'm not here to hurt you!' he shouted. 'So stop trying to hurt me! Listen, if the sheriff and his deputies find you, they'll arrest you! You got that? Arrest you and lock you away in a mental hospital! You don't want that to happen, do you?'

The only response was a miniature rockslide, a whole bunch of small rocks and pebbles suddenly rolling down the sloping canyon wall, gathering momentum, bouncing, tumbling ever faster —

One smacked into the rear fender with

enough force to make the vehicle sway.

'Aw, Jesus! Cut it out, will you? What's wrong with you? Why won't you let me help you?'

He heard an odd sound then, a weird, low, whirring that he couldn't immediately identify. A moment later a rock came pitching over the ridge, describing a wider arc than the rest and travelling noticeably faster. It punched into the VW's windshield, leaving a whitish crater in the glass from which a dozen cracks immediately fanned out.

He frowned. *What the hell . . . ?*

Again he heard that peculiar whirring sound, and a few seconds later another rock came plunging out of thin air to smash into the VW's roof.

Crouching low, mind racing, Mitch thought, *If I didn't know better . . . I'd say she's got some kind of a sling up there. That she's using a sling to fire rocks down on me.*

Diana's voice suddenly interrupted his thoughts.

'All you want is the gold!' she screamed. Her words bounced off the canyon walls, seeming to amplify her fury.

Mitch sighed. 'Sure I want the gold. So do Agnes and Scottie. But that doesn't mean I won't help you. Listen, Diana . . . you've got to trust me. Aggie does. That's why she told me where to find you! So I could help you!'

'How would you help me?' she replied angrily. 'By offering me a deal? I tell you where the gold's buried and you turn me over to the sheriff? Is that it?'

'No! You're way off base. If you come with me, I'll hide you. You'll be safe.'

The canyon fell quiet again, and he wondered if she'd lit out while he was speaking.

'Diana,' he called. 'Trust me. I'm not lying, I swear!'

But again there was only silence.

* * *

As soon as they got back to the house, Scott tended to Kelly-Anne's scratches.

He'd been searching the far end of the canyon when he'd heard the far-off blare of the Camaro's horn, and thinking that

Kelly-Anne had found Diana he'd immediately turned and jogged back the way he'd come.

But when the car finally came into sight, he saw only Kelly-Anne standing beside it and he'd felt an angry stab of disappointment.

Then he drew close enough to see the state of her . . . the scratches, the blood. He hurried up to her. 'Jesus, Kell', what happened to — ?'

She slapped him, hard.

'What the fuck was *that* for?'

'For dumping me in this fucking wilderness!'

'I didn't dump you. You wanted to come, remember?' His tone softened. 'Now tell me what happened.'

Wanting very badly to slap him again, she said, 'What happened? I tell you what happened! Your sister's fucking cat tried to tear me apart, *that's* what happened!'

'Benji?' He looked around, baffled. 'Out here?'

'Yes, goddammit, out here!' Before he could reply, she added, 'Now get in the car and take me back to the house! I've

191

had enough of this business, Scott, and I've had enough of *you!*'

'But what about the gold?'

'What gold? For all you know there *isn't* any gold!'

Scott opened his mouth to say more, but then shut it again. Once Kelly-Anne had made up her mind, no one could change it. Forcing himself to calm down, he opened the door for her, then went around and climbed in behind the wheel and drove off.

No-one was around when they let themselves into the house forty minutes later. They went straight to the kitchen and Scott dug antiseptic and Band-Aids from one of the cabinets. Kelly-Anne sat stiffly while he carefully cleaned and treated her shoulders and face, patching her up as best he could. She stared directly ahead, unblinking, her mouth firmed tight. She was in a foul mood, and the hell of it was that he could hardly blame her.

Afterwards they went upstairs and packed their cases in silence. Scott threw them into the trunk while Kelly-Anne settled herself in the passenger seat, still stubbornly quiet.

'I'll go find Agnes and tell her we're leaving,' he said.

Kelly-Anne ignored him.

He went back into the house, wondering for the first time where Agnes and Mitch — especially Mitch — had gotten to. He climbed the stairs and knocked at Agnes's closed bedroom door.

There was no response, but he knew she was in there because he could hear the soft strains of some classical piece issuing from her radio.

'Agnes?'

No answer. He tried the door handle, found the door locked and swore softly.

'Agnes, I know you're in there!'

Silence.

He shrugged. 'Well, we're going now. Kelly's had another run-in with one of those feral cats you were talking about, and I'm taking her home. You hear me? We're leaving now.'

More silence.

'Agnes! Do you hear me? Open the door!'

He shook his head, thinking, *What a dysfunctional fucking family*. In his bleaker moments he often thought they were all as crazy as each other.

'For the last time, sis, we're leaving. That's what you wanted, isn't it? Don't you want to say good-bye?' he added.

Still no answer.

'Agnes, for chrissake talk to me!'

Angrily he punched the door, then turned and hurried downstairs.

'I can't believe I let her kick me out again,' he said when he climbed into the car beside Kelly-Anne. 'That gold's mine, dammit. *Mine!*'

'Maybe it is,' she said sullenly. 'But first you have to prove that it exists.'

'Oh, it's here! Goddammit, I know it's here!'

'Then sue the bitch. Threaten to drag her through court. Maybe the thought of having to drive back and forth to the city every day'll make her change her mind.'

'That,' he said, grinning, 'is not a bad idea.'

She made a vague gesture with her scratched hands. 'Whatever. Right now, just get us out of here. I've had enough of this dump. Besides, I want to get a tetanus shot before these damn scratches get infected.'

Scott's mind was already forging ahead, thinking about the threat of legal proceedings and how Agnes would sooner cave in than risk having to set foot outside and show up in court. Glancing one final time at Kelly-Anne, he decided that she'd had her uses after all.

He drove up the rise, away from the house. Still bitter, he drove aggressively and much faster than was safe. The headlights showed him the trail ahead, but anything beyond that cone of light was lost in the unrelieved blackness of the desert night.

'Are you sure you couldn't find anything about her to indicate mental illness?' he asked. 'That would strengthen our case.'

'In my professional opinion,' Kelly-Anne replied wearily, mechanically, 'she's as sane as you or I. Which may not be saying much.'

'Oh, she may *seem* normal. Even to

someone with your training. But behind that façade there's a dangerous schizophrenic capable of anything. Even murder.'

Kelly-Anne shot him a look. 'You saying you think she killed Neon?'

He was about to reply when something small and dark suddenly slammed against the windshield. The heavy thump scared the shit out of them. Startled, Scott fought the wheel. Managing to keep the car under control, he turned his attention to the road but found his view obscured —

Obscured by Benji.

He realised then that the cat had deliberately jumped out of nowhere onto the car; that it was glaring at them, copper eyes burning with hatred; and that as crazy as it sounded Benji looked as if he wanted nothing more than to see them dead.

Scott heard the high-pitched, feral sound the cat made as it hissed at them, and then —

Then he lost control of the car.

It seemed to slide away beneath him, and for some indefinable reason he didn't seem able to stop it. As it slewed and fishtailed and finally left the road and bumped and jolted over rougher ground toward some rocks thirty feet away, he stamped on the brake.

Nothing happened; the car just kept ploughing forward, the needle still touching seventy.

The car filled with his and Kelly-Anne's screams. Outside, Benji raked his claws down the windshield and snarled his evil, feral chirrup.

The rocks loomed menacingly up before them. At the last moment Benji leaped off the hood and into the surrounding darkness. An instant later the Camaro smashed nose-first into the rocks. Scott and Kelly-Anne were hurled forward, through the glass.

The hood crumpled and the impact of the collision rammed the engine block back into the car. It crushed Scott and Kelly-Anne. They were already unconscious when the vehicle exploded in a fireball. Fiery debris rained over the desert.

Crouched on a rock Benji watched with cool approval as the car and its occupants burned to death, then he slunk away into the night.

★ ★ ★

Finally reaching the end of his patience, Mitch broke cover, looked up toward the now barely-discernible ridge above and yelled, 'Okay, you win! I'm going! Happy now?'

Nothing.

'You can take your chances with the sheriff!'

He took one last look around, instinct telling him that Diana was still up there somewhere. Then he climbed back into the beat-up VW, gunned the engine, turned on the lights and reversed back the way he'd come.

He backed up about a quarter of a mile, then stopped and killed the engine and lights. Awkwardly, because his ankle was giving him hell again, he got out and quietly limped back toward Diana's hiding-place.

I must be crazy, he thought as he began to climb up the steep rocky slope. *What's the use of all that gold if I go and break my freaking neck?*

Even before he got halfway to the top he had to pause and catch his breath. The early evening was already turning cold, but his shirt was plastered to him. He wiped away the sweat and was just about to continue his ascent when he heard a soft, ominous sound.

A cat, chirruping in the darkness above him.

An unpleasant tingle washed through him. He quickly grabbed up a rock. But as he did so the near-silence returned and the darkness ahead seemed to empty of threat.

He tossed the rock away and doggedly continued upward. The moon appeared from behind the drifting clouds and in the half-light he was just able to make out the mouth of a cave twenty feet above him.

He needed to rest, but also wanted to get this confrontation over, so he forced himself to keep searching out hand- and footholds, dragging himself higher and trying not to think about falling. It took great effort but ten sweaty minutes later he hauled himself up onto the ledge fronting the cave.

This had better be worth it, he thought.

He wearily got to his feet, heart thudding, and as he turned toward the cave-mouth he sensed rather than saw a flicker of movement in the darkness.

Suddenly something came flying out at him, something long and loose like a heavy length of rope.

It struck him in the chest. He grabbed at it, felt its scales rippling against his palms and realised it wasn't rope at all, it was a snake.

It struggled in his grip, hissing angrily. He stepped back and was about to hurl the snake away when he realised that he'd run out of ledge. Suddenly he was falling . . .

He hit the rocky slope painfully hard and bounced and rolled, tumbling over and over, plunging into a dark and seemingly bottomless pit.

He struck his head on a rock and everything went black. When he came around he found himself sprawled on his back and his swollen left ankle wedged between two jagged rocks. Dazed, he waited for the cobwebs to leave his brain; then took a deep breath. A sharp pain knifed through his bruised chest and wondered if he'd broken a rib. The star-spattered sky seemed to cartwheel above him.

Then he heard an angry hiss beside him.

Ignoring the pain and the urge to puke, he craned his neck and saw that the snake Diana had thrown at him — a rattler as long as his leg — had landed no more than a few inches from the top of his head. It lay curled, ready to strike.

Desperately Mitch tried to free his ankle from between the two rocks. It was impossible.

He was stuck.

Christ, oh Christ —

The snake reared its head back. But even as it prepared to strike, Mitch heard someone land softly beside him and say gently: 'No . . . '

The rattler froze.

Mitch dragged his eyes from the snake and saw a shadowy figure step closer to him.

It was Diana.

She crouched beside him, a wild, beautiful, spiteful, gorgeous thing, her body golden, smooth, all fine lines and perfect curves, her black, tangled hair standing out wildly around her face, her eyes —

Her eyes had the same almond shape as those of a cat.

Kneeling, she put her face close to the snake, and repeated softly: 'No . . . '

Holding his breath, Mitch watched in amazement as the snake seemed to calm and lower its head, almost in subservience. A moment later it slithered away.

Diana slowly got to her feet. In the moonlight she looked magnificent. She peered down at him for a moment, from above the challenging thrust of her breasts; and then, as suddenly as she had appeared, she was gone.

Mitch sat up and ignoring the pain in his chest and ankle, yelled for her to come back.

But she'd already disappeared.

He sagged, drew a painful breath and then gingerly eased his leg from between the two rocks. The pain made him sweat. He examined the swollen ankle to make sure nothing was broken. Now more than ever he wanted to go after her, but in his condition he knew it was useless. Brushing himself off, he glanced around to get his bearings and then limped slowly back toward the VW.

He was almost there when she tried to run him down.

The first he knew of it was the building growl of the engine. Then the headlights flared over him. Cursing, he spun around, shielded his eyes from the light — and then the pickup, the same red pickup that had nearly turned him into road-kill just a few days earlier, was almost on top of him.

He dived aside, hitting the ground and rolling over, the pain from his many injuries making him cry out.

Moments later the pickup was gone.

Furious, he dragged himself up and glared after the truck. All he could see was the dust settling. Dammit, that was twice she'd tried to run him over. Determined not to let her get away with it a second time, he limped back to the VW. As he started to open the door, he saw that the nearside front tire had been slashed.

Goddamn her! He angrily punched the roof of the car with both fists and swore with a savagery that surprised even him. He then limped to the trunk and reached for the spare. His hands felt something sticky and he quickly drew them back.

What the . . . ?

He inspected his palms in the half-light. They were covered with a waxy brown substance, the same substance Crane had found on the pitchfork handle.

Wiping his palms on his pants, Mitch grabbed the spare and set about changing the flat.

11

It was almost midnight when he got back to the Oasis. The temperature had cooled dramatically and the house was in darkness. As he got out of the VW he looked around for Scott's Camaro. It was gone. He wondered if Scott and Kelly-Anne had finally decided to cut their losses and quit.

Almost beyond caring, he let himself indoors, heard classical music coming from Agnes's room and dragged himself slowly up the stairs toward it.

'Aggie! Aggie, you up there?'

Agnes's door was ajar. The bedroom was dark. Mitch peered inside, saw light showing under the closed bathroom door and heard the shower going.

He entered, knocked on the bathroom door and called out: 'Agnes? It's me — Mitch.'

'Be right out, sweetheart.' He heard the water stop. 'There's wine on the bedside cabinet. Why don't you pour us both a glass?'

He frowned.

Both of us?

Hobbling to the table, he filled two glasses and took his own to the pink couch in the corner. He pushed several stuffed cats to the far end, then sank down with a grateful sigh, sipped the wine and closed his eyes.

Shortly the bathroom door opened and Agnes came out, silhouetted by the light.

Mitch opened his eyes and caught his breath.

She was wearing a wispy little square of near-transparent pink chiffon, and the body he could see outlined beneath it was close to perfection.

Aroused, he looked her over. Her pale breasts were high and perfectly symmetrical, each one tipped by a small pink nipple. She narrowed gracefully at the waist, and as she stood there for his inspection her legs looked longer, more slender and supple than he ever would have guessed.

'You like?' she asked softly.

Only her ever-present white gloves spoiled the vision, but he let that pass. 'Are you kidding? What's not to like?'

She joined him on the couch and snuggled up to him. 'I'm glad,' she whispered. 'I want so much to please you.'

She started to kiss him but pulled back when she saw all his cuts and bruises. 'Oh my God, what happened?'

'Guess.'

'Diana,' she said flatly.

'The bitch tried to kill me. First with rocks and then with a goddamn snake. Then she tried to run me over with her truck — the same fucking truck she tried to run me over with before I even *got* here.'

'Oh dear God . . . '

'That ain't the weirdest part,' he added. 'I lost my footing and fell, got my damn foot stuck between two rocks and the snake's just about to bite me when she stops it. Says 'No,' and the frigging thing just crawls away . . . ' He eyed Agnes grimly. 'I mean, who can talk to snakes?'

Closing his eyes, he held the glass

against his forehead hoping to ease the pain.

'You poor baby,' Agnes said. 'You must be exhausted.'

He nodded. 'Did Sherlock come back?'

'Sheriff Crane, you mean? No. No, he didn't.'

'Well, he *will*. And sooner rather than later, if I know that sonofabitch.'

'Shhh, darling. Don't worry about him now.'

Rising, she came close and straddled him. She smelled fresh, clean and sexy. He loved the feel of her weight on him, of her groin resting against his, of feeling himself harden against her.

'Maybe if I go out again early tomorrow,' he said as she gently massaged his temples, 'before Crane and his guys get here . . .'

'They'll never find Diana,' Agnes said. 'No-one will. They might just as well chase a ghost.'

She pulled his head down between her scented breasts. 'Just so you're all right. That's all that matters to me.'

He nuzzled her, wondering what she

was going to be like, whether or not she was still a virgin.

'You *do* love me, don't you?' she whispered.

'Sure.'

'I mean, you don't just want me for the gold?'

'I'm starting to believe there isn't any gold.'

'But even if there was, it's still *me* you want most, isn't it?'

'Yes,' he said. He kissed each of her breasts.

'Promise?'

'Promise.'

He felt her sigh with relief. 'Oh, sweetheart,' she said, 'we're going to have such a wonderful life together. Just the three of us . . . '

'Three?'

She smiled down at him.

'Of course. You . . . me . . . and Benji.'

He realised then that one of the stuffed cats occupying the window sill was actually the real thing. It purred contentedly as it looked out over the sleeping desert. Mitch realised that it had been there, watching him, watching them, all this time.

He thought uneasily, *Yeah. The three of us.*

* * *

She was surprisingly good, considering that she told him it was her first time. She threw herself into it, determined to enjoy everything he could offer, and as tired and beaten as he was, he found her excitement contagious.

They made a good team, he told himself as he felt her tighten her legs around him and almost shed tears as she reached her first orgasm. But did he *really* love her? How *could* he? He hardly knew her.

Afterwards he lay awake in the darkness and listened to the soft sounds she made sleeping, and thought about the gold. Where could it be? Where could Flapjack have buried it?

Where would I have buried it? he wondered. He thought long and hard, but still came up empty.

Dammit, Diana knows.

Neon knew.

Neon . . .

He turned his head, watched Agnes's peaceful profile for a moment. Then, slowly, quietly, so as not to wake her, he got out of bed.

He went into the bathroom and closed the door. As he was stepping into his jeans, he accidentally knocked a spray can off a shelf beside the washbasin. He caught it before it could hit the floor and quietly returned it to the shelf. Finished dressing, he left the bathroom, silently crossed the bedroom and let himself out.

Still limping, he climbed the trail to the snake-farm, his breathing loud in the silence of the cold desert night. Hobbling around to the diner, he let himself inside and picked his way through to Neon's storeroom-home.

Inside, by the weird flickering light of the old neon signs, he turned out drawers and checked shelves, looking for anything that might give him the clue he was searching for. He dragged an old suitcase out from beneath the futon, opened it and rummaged through a jumble of old

211

clothes, a few faded snapshots.

Nothing.

He swore, but kept digging. At last he found a couple of old letters, and then a receipt from a garden supply store, dated two weeks earlier.

He tilted it to the light and read:

LIME — 6 BAGS
CHARGE TO
MISS AGNES SHELBY

He thought: *What did you need lime for, Neon?*

Lime . . .

He noticed then that something had been hand-written on the reverse side of the receipt. It took a few moments but finally he managed to decipher the almost illegible scrawl:

KEEP IN CASE
SHE TRIES TO
FRAME YOU

Tucking the receipt into his shirt pocket, Mitch slid the case back under the bed. He took a final look around, then switched off the lights and left the room.

He was just limping back through the gutted kitchen area when he heard a sudden humming sound that made him pause. He glanced around, and after a moment realised that it was coming from beneath a large, blanket-covered object set against the right-side wall.

He approached it warily, crunching dirt and debris underfoot, and lifted the edge of the blanket.

Beneath it sat an oblong-shaped chest freezer.

It was the only thing in the room that was plugged in and working. For some unknown reason the sight of it made his throat go dry, his pulse quicken.

Although he had a bad feeling about this, he knew he had to take a look inside, if only to tell himself that he was wrong.

He turned on the light switch. A single, dust-covered fluorescent light strip ticked briefly and then flickered to life.

Swallowing his apprehension, he curled his fingers under the edge of the freezer lid and lifted it.

A smoky white vapour ghosted lazily toward the ceiling.

Ah Jesus . . .

He rocked backwards, shock leaving him giddy, and he swallowed several times to prevent himself from throwing up.

A woman's body had been laid out in the bottom of the otherwise-empty freezer, and then covered with lime. The corrosive had already started to work, and now she was little more than half-body, half-bone. Chunks of flesh had been eaten away along her arms and legs, her hips, one breast, and of course her face.

Diana's once-beautiful face.

Another wave of nausea swept over him as he breathed in the harsh, caustic air, and he dropped the lid.

Diana was dead. She'd been dead at least a week, probably longer, if the date on the receipt was any indicator.

But if you're dead, he thought, *who's out there in the desert? Who tried to kill me tonight, and then saved me from the snake?*

Gagging, he stumbled outside to get

some fresh air, desperately trying to slow his runaway mind, to bring order back to his thoughts and review everything that had happened up to this point.

All the facts were there, he knew, but they were so jumbled up that nothing made sense.

Then, unaccountably, he suddenly recalled something Neon had said about Flapjack Shelby the previous night.

'Last I saw, he was drivin' up the slope toward those rocks. You know them rocks, where the girls' pets're buried?'

Mitch's taut expression slackened.

Of course — the graves!

He limped around to the tool shed, ripped open the bloodstained door and grabbed a long-handled shovel. Then, ignoring the protests of his aching body, he worked his way around the hollow and came to the rock-sheltered pet cemetery from above.

He stopped by the first wooden cross, clamped his mouth hard and started to dig. It was hard painful work, but he kept at it because he knew he was close now, close enough to almost *smell* the fortune that he was sure awaited him.

Again and again the blade of the shovel bit into the earth. Again and again he levered out one great clod after another and tossed them aside.

Dig, lever, throw, dig, lever, throw . . .

He worked like a man possessed, a man driven by a lust that was almost as old as time itself, a special kind of lust that only gold could stir.

At last he struck something hollow and wooden. He froze. Discarding the shovel, he dropped to his knees and started scraping away the dirt with his hands, digging deeper and deeper.

At last his fingernails raked against some sort of lid. He swore as damp, dirt-darkened splinters jabbed into his fingertips. He cleared more dirt, finally uncovered a homemade box roughly eighteen inches by twelve and dragged it from the hole.

Breathing hard, he wiped the lid free of dirt, examined it quickly and then used the blade of the shovel to pry it loose.

The lid broke free with a loud wrenching of rusty nails. He threw it away. Inside the box lay the dry, skeletal remains of a long-dead cat.

He cursed.

Reaching inside, he grabbed the skeleton and would have tossed it aside if it hadn't crumbled in his grasp. The small, delicate bones fell apart and turned to powder. Ignoring them, he felt around in the shadowy bottom of the box.

He stopped when his fingers touched something cool and soft.

He gripped the object and pulled it out, saw with a frown that it was a small leather pouch, drawn tight at the neck by a strip of rawhide. Curious, he untied the rawhide, opened the neck of the pouch and emptied its contents into his palm.

He stared at a mixture of nuggets and gold dust.

Excitement rushed through him. He chuckled to himself, then delved back into the little homemade coffin and brought out seven more pouches.

I've found it! Oh Christ on a cross, I've actually found it!

He stacked the pouches against the rocks behind him and then stumbled to his feet. *Flapjack*, he thought. *You crafty old bastard!*

Too excited to think straight, he looked around, selected another grave and began digging with the shovel. Dig, lever, throw, dig, lever, throw —

Suddenly, the earth at his feet gave way and the hole he'd been digging collapsed in on itself. Remembering what Neon had said about sinkholes he tried to step back, but in that same moment something brushed hard against his calves. Losing his balance, he fell forward, his arms windmilling.

He tumbled some ten feet into a narrow, funnel-shaped pit. He landed, hard, his right leg twisted under him, and lay there dazed and confused, as loose dirt poured down from above, choking him.

Gagging, he fought off the rising panic and tried to get up. But something was wrong, something was *badly* wrong, because he couldn't seem to move his legs . . .

He sat up, his world a tilting, tipping, unstable place, and saw by moonlight that his legs were already half-buried beneath a mound of fallen dirt. He struggled to free himself and screamed when he finally managed to move a little and realised from the stab of agony in his right leg that it was broken.

All at once the gold was the least of his concerns. Dirt was still pouring down on top of him, filling the narrow grave-shaped pit into which he'd fallen, and a panicky voice in his mind was telling him that he was going to *die* down here. If he didn't get some help, he was actually going to *die* . . .

More dirt tumbled down on him, clogging his nose and throat. He kept his eyes shut and tried to spit out the dirt in his mouth, but more forced its way in. He started to choke; then, above the sound of his own coughing, he heard something above him.

A menacing chirrup.

He looked up, even as another cascade of dirt collapsed on him, and through the smothering dust saw Benji peering down at him, his copper eyes devoid of emotion.

He realised then it was Benji who'd

brushed against his calves, Benji who'd made him lose his balance, Benji who was intent on killing him.

Suddenly he heard a voice calling his name and he sobbed with relief.

'Agnes!' he screamed. 'Down here!'

A few moments later she appeared, standing beside the cat at the edge of the pit and staring down at him.

Only it wasn't Agnes, any more than it was Diana.

It was a weird mixture of the two.

She wore Agnes's familiar white gloves and tinted glasses, but she also wore Diana's Daisy Duke cutoffs and Diana's thin top.

In places her skin was pale, almost translucent, just like Agnes's, but in others it was streaked with Diana's deep, coppery skin-tone.

And the hair . . .

Agnes' honey-blonde hair showed plainly beneath the black wig she'd pulled over it.

Agnes . . .

A lot of things suddenly became clear to him and he thought of the spray can he'd almost knocked over but just managed to catch.

Fake tan . . .

The same greasy brown substance Crane had found on the handle of the pitchfork that killed Neon.

'Agnes . . . ' he said. 'For chrissake . . . '

The woman who was both Agnes and Diana began to cry.

'D-Diana was right,' Agnes wept. 'She *said* you didn't really love me! Said all you were interested in was *her* . . . and the *gold!*'

He shook his head. 'No, no, honey . . . you've got it all wrong!' He spit out a mouthful of dirt, adding desperately: 'Listen to me! I need help! You got to get a rope and pull me out of here!'

'Why? So you can go off with Diana and leave me all by myself? So that you can take Papa's gold and squander it?'

'Agnes,' he begged. 'Diana's dead. You killed her, didn't you? You and Neon? B-because you knew she was going to tell Scott where the gold w-was buried?'

She smiled down at him, a vacant, distracted, pointless kind of smile that chilled him to the bone.

'*I'm* Diana now,' she said. 'I can be

Diana any time I want.'

He tried to humour her. 'Okay. Okay, h-honey. We . . . we'll talk about it later. J-just get me out of here now. I've busted my leg.'

'Oh, no . . . '

'What?'

'No,' she repeated firmly. 'You lied to me, Mitch. You lied to Agnes, broke your promise. You didn't want her. All you wanted was Diana and the gold!'

'That's not true!' he screamed. 'Sure I wanted the gold! But I wanted it for *us!* You and me!'

'Liar! You didn't want me. You wanted Diana. You *always* wanted Diana. She told me so. But I told *her* something, too.'

She peeled off the white gloves and threw them aside. Her hands were smooth, untouched by allergy. She picked up the fallen shovel and glared at him. 'I told her that I'd kill you rather than let her have you.'

'No!' he begged. 'Agnes, for chrissake, no! Please!'

'Yes,' she said, starting to cry again. 'Yes.'

She began to shovel dirt on top of him.

She didn't stop again for a very long time.

★   ★   ★

When it was done and the hole was filled in and she could no longer hear his begging screams, she stabbed the shovel into the earth like a temporary marker, then turned and headed down the slope toward the house.

She was lifeless now. In her hastily-donned wig and tear-streaked face that was striped with alternate lines of Agnes's white skin and Diana's tan, her expression was devoid off all emotion.

She entered the house, thinking how convenient it was for everyone to believe she was agoraphobic. Poor little neurotic Agnes, who'd always been overlooked and forced to live in her sister's larger shadow — she's never done anything because she can't even leave the house.

As she approached the stairs, Benji, trotting beside her, suddenly gave a low, warning chirrup.

223

A voice said softly from the darkness on her left: 'I've been waiting for you.'

Agnes stopped and turned slowly toward the den.

'Who's there?'

'Come on in and find out,' invited the voice.

She walked forward and paused in the doorway.

'Turn the light on.'

Agnes obeyed. Dull light from the two brass chandeliers showed a man sitting in the over-stuffed armchair facing the door.

''Evening, Miss Agnes,' said Sheriff Crane. 'Or is it Miss Diana? Hard to tell which one you are tonight.'

Agnes looked at him through dead, dangerous eyes.

'Looks to me like you've been busy.' He sat with his legs crossed, covering her with his Glock 22.40.

She stared at him, speechless.

'Come in,' he repeated. 'Don't be shy. Sit down. We need to talk, you and me.'

'About what?'

'Diana, of course. And why you and Neon killed her.'

Again, she stared at him in silence.

'About why you tried to live her life as well as your own and then killed Neon, your brother and his wife, and then Mitch Akins. But most of all, Miss Agnes, we need to talk about what's going to happen *next*. And about the gold.'

She came deeper into the room, sat down on the sofa across from him, her movements mechanical, lifeless. She was streaked with dust and dirt and sweat. Wearily she pulled the black wig from her head.

'How long have you known?'

He shrugged one beefy shoulder. 'Almost from the start. Your story about the burglar . . . there were too many inconsistencies.'

'Such as?'

'By your own admission, your boyfriend — uh, my apologies, Miss Agnes, your *fiancé* — arrived 'shortly after' the perp managed to escape. And yet when I asked him about it, Akins said the perp was 'long gone' by the time he got here.'

He paused to let his words sink in.

'Then there was Benji. You told me

he'd been missing all day. So who left the ball on the stairs, the ball that Akins — the burglar — slipped on?'

'I've no idea.'

'There were other things, too,' he continued. 'Your description of the burglar, for instance. Short, stocky, fair hair, round face — the exact opposite of the *real* perp. A broken mop-handle I found, a blood-stained length of wood that both suddenly went missing about the same time someone — *you* — tried to introduce me to a black-tailed rattler. By themselves they didn't mean much. But added together, well, they just set me to thinking.'

'So you're going to arrest me now, is that it?' she asked.

He paused momentarily before shaking his head. 'No, Miss Agnes,' he replied almost gently. 'I'm going to help you.'

She frowned.

'You've gotten yourself into a heck of a mess out here. Seems to me that only someone with a strong background in law enforcement, who knows the system and how it works, can get you out of it.'

'You?'

'Me,' he confirmed. 'And I can do it, too. There are ways and means by which we can explain all this away and make sure no one ever guesses the truth.'

'And why would you want to do that?'

The gun in his grip wavered briefly.

'I lost my wife three years ago,' he said grimly. 'And there hasn't been a day since that I haven't wanted to join her. I loved my wife very much, Miss Agnes. I *still* love her. And I miss her so bad that sometimes, most times, I ache with it.

'Well, I'm tired of that ache. I'm tired of grieving and not knowing what to do to make it all better, of killing time and just waiting to die so I can be with her again, and before you ask, no: I won't kill myself because I know Mabel wouldn't approve of that. So I figure to serve out what time I have left as sheriff — if they'll let me, that is, which is looking increasingly unlikely — and then shake the dust of this county, of this state, of this *country*, if I have to, from my heels.'

'Where will you go?'

'I'm not sure right now. I figure to travel, see: to settle down somewhere I can find some peace until my time *does* come. But to do that, I'll need money. More than I'll get from my pension.'

'In other words, you want the gold.'

'Not all of it. I'm not greedy. Just enough to make my life comfortable.'

'And in return . . . ?'

'I'll make all this trouble go away, guaranteed. I'll bury it, just the way *you* buried Mitch Akins.'

She considered the suggestion, asked finally, 'How much do you want?'

'Half.'

'Do I have any choice in the matter?'

'Nope.'

She inclined her head, her fingers fidgeting nervously with the black wig. 'Then it seems we have a deal,' she said flatly.

He stood up and put the gun away. 'I hoped you'd be sensible, Miss Agnes. I mean, there's plenty for both of us, right?'

She didn't answer.

'I'll show myself out,' he told her. 'But I'll be back sometime within the next week or so, once I've set some wheels in motion, taken care of things.'

'I'll be here. And for what it's worth, sheriff, I give you my word that you'll get what you want in return.'

When he was gone, and his car had driven off down the driveway, she looked at Benji who was licking his paws at her feet. 'Oh, Benji,' she said. 'My wonderful, beautiful Benji . . .'

The big grey cat looked at her with his eerie, coppery eyes.

Scooping him up in her arms, she said, 'I meant it, you know. Once he's served his purpose, we'll give him *exactly* what he wants, you and me. But don't worry. It won't be Papa's gold. Oh, no. Sheriff Crane doesn't really want that, does he? Of course not. All he wants is to be reunited with his wife.'

She nuzzled the cat's soft head, and he purred with pleasure. 'I think we can arrange that, don't you?'

Benji blinked once.

'I'll take that as a yes,' she whispered.

Benji purred a little louder, and rubbed the top of his head against her chin.

THE END

We do hope that you have enjoyed reading this large print book.

Did you know that all of our titles are available for purchase?

We publish a wide range of high quality large print books including:
Romances, Mysteries, Classics
General Fiction
Non Fiction and Westerns

Special interest titles available in large print are:
The Little Oxford Dictionary
Music Book, Song Book
Hymn Book, Service Book

Also available from us courtesy of Oxford University Press:
Young Readers' Dictionary
(large print edition)
Young Readers' Thesaurus
(large print edition)

For further information or a free brochure, please contact us at:
Ulverscroft Large Print Books Ltd.,
The Green, Bradgate Road, Anstey,
Leicester, LE7 7FU, England.
Tel: (00 44) **0116 236 4325**
Fax: (00 44) **0116 234 0205**

MYSTERY OF THE CRATER

John Glasby

Brander, the security chief of the Syrtis Base on Mars, isolates the entire emplacement when two men die from an unknown, alien disease. No one can enter or leave the base. Dr. John Naysmith, newly arrived on Mars, leads the medical team desperately trying discover a serum to combat the virus. If they can't contain the spread of the disease Brander must annihilate the base and everyone in it with nuclear bombs! Then another three men became infected . . .

DR. MORELLE'S CASEBOOK

Ernest Dudley

After a spate of time-wasting telephone calls, the Doctor had told Miss Frayle not to bother him with them; she must dismiss the callers and leave him to work on his thesis. But when the telephone rang again it was Professor Howard, clearly in the midst of a desperate struggle, wanting to speak to the Doctor on a matter of life and death. The Professor was being attacked — by spiders. So begins one of Doctor Morelle's strangest cases . . .

MIRACLE MAN

John Russell Fearn

When the President elect of the Bureau of Advanced Science, Dr. Mark Haslam, encounters Esau Jones, he's astonished to learn that Jones can perform apparent miracles. Yet, despite his amazing gifts, Jones is content to remain anonymous, living the life of a country rustic. Haslam, however, persuades Jones to leave his preferred anonymity and rural life, to demonstrate his powers before the Bureau of Advanced Science in London. But there he makes a very dangerous enemy of Dr. Carfax . . .

TANNER'S GUNS

Matt Logan

It's 1913. Mexico is being torn apart by revolution and the rebels need guns to oust the corrupt General Huerta in Mexico City. Elliott Blaze has an entire arsenal for sale. All he needs is trustworthy, Spanish-speaking Jake Tanner to get a tough job done . . . However, Jake and his partner in crime are soon playing cat-and-mouse with the armies of two countries. They've been double-crossed, and now face a terrifying showdown, pitted against the Mexican Army's latest secret weapon!